# A CHRISTMAS IN TIME

## *Christmas, 1799*

*Book Three of The Oldest House Series*

BY

## DEBORAH L. COURVILLE

THE SAMOTHRACE PRESS, LTD.

A portion of the proceeds from the sale of all books in The Oldest House Series will be donated to The Oldest House, Laceyville, Pennsylvania, for its upkeep and repair. The Oldest House is a living museum and registered non profit 501 (c) (3). It is staffed and run entirely by volunteers. It relies on grants and generous donations from the public for its survival.

# ABOUT THE AUTHOR

The author of 'A Christmas in Time,' Deborah L. Courville, is a volunteer at The Oldest House (built 1781) in Laceyville, Wyoming County, PA. Like her protagonist 'Izzy' she was a journalist for a local newspaper for several years, and is descended from French nobility.

Courville lives just outside Laceyville on Doolittle Hill, where she moved more than two decades ago. She holds a Ph.D. in Linguistics & English, enjoys history, languages, music and science, and is an intrepid and inveterate traveler.

In addition to leading tours (usually in period garb) at The Oldest House, Courville curates the Period Clothing Display there, which features authentic items from the 1770's through the early 1920's. She has found historic costuming a new passion and delight.

Courville has always been intrigued by the concept of time travel. Though a mediaevalist by scholarship and natural inclination, she became fascinated by the Colonial and post Colonial period of the United States when she started volunteering at The Oldest House a few years ago.

'A Christmas in Time' is the third book in **The Oldest House Series,** which began with the highly acclaimed 'A River in Time.'

Under the pen name 'Eugénie D. West' Courville is also the author of a series of best-selling murder mysteries.

**Visit Courville on Twitter at @LadyCourville, on Facebook at Deborah de Billy dit Courville, and on her blog, 'Lacing up a Modern Woman: Adventures in the 18th Century' at DLC18thcentury.blogspot.com**

**Or, as Eugénie D. West on Twitter at @EugenieDWest, on Facebook at Eugenie D. West, and on her blog, 'The Books of Eugenie D. West' at Thebooksofeugniedwest.blogspot.com**

## A Note of Thanks

*I am continually grateful for the help, tutelage and support given to me by the other active volunteers at the Oldest House. I have been so honored to be a part of this, and hope to carry on for many years to come.*

*Thank you also to the Pastor and People of the Braintrim Baptist Church for your welcoming encouragement.*

# INTRODUCTION

This is a work of fiction.

I must state that once again because, the more involved I become with my own creatures Izzy and Josh, and the historical Braintrim and its actual residents of the late 18th century, the more details I found needed to be part of this book. In many cases, verifiable historical documentation was either non existent or woefully inadequate. I thus came to rely on what I call 'informed imagining.'

As with anything, the more I learned about the very late 18th and very early 19th century, the more I realized how little I knew during this, my third trip back in time, as it were.

In the late winter of 1799, several events were taking place in the U.S., in Braintrim Pennsylvania, and in the world. The Alien and Sedition Acts were seeing newspaper editors who did not agree with the Federalist point of view vilified, terrorized and in some cases run out of town (or to their deaths).

The XYZ Affair had left a very bad taste in most citizens' mouths, and President Adams' bid for a second term in the 1800 election seemed less and less likely to succeed.

The slave revolt in the Caribbean, sparked by the French Revolution in 1789, would affect not only global trade, but the practice of slavery here at home: New York State abolished slavery in the middle of 1799, and the subject became a crucial one in a few decades at the start of the U.S. Civil War.

A disagreement over property rights had caused a schism in the Braintrim Baptist Church, one that would not be healed for more than a decade.

Beethoven and Haydn were composing, electricity was being rudimentarily harnessed, the Napoleonic Wars were draining the coffers of France while 'the Little Emperor' became Dictator, and George Washington died.

All of these things as well as others referred to in this book are documented, verifiable, historical events.

What was the most fun, and the greatest challenge in this book, was to imagine how the people of Braintrim in 1799 might have heard about and reacted to these events. What might they have thought about the political atmosphere in the nation and the globe? of the French? of slavery? of Beethoven and Haydn? of local troubles?

Although I did my level best to be historically accurate, there were times when I had to bend the prism of history to align with the story line: for that, I apologize and hope to be forgiven.

But, as I have said before: this is a work of fiction.

I advanced the actual date of the Rev. Samuel Sturdevant, Sr.'s marriage to Ann-Lucy Brown Cooley by a year, and also the births of their children accordingly so the timeline of the series would work. Because I was not always able to find primary source material to document deaths or birth dates for historical personages, I estimated or omitted these where necessary.

Many of the characters in this book did actually live in Braintrim and northeastern Pennsylvania in 1799. However, we have no sources that tell us what these people were really like. While I am certain it would be comforting to think that they were all pure gold through and through, that would make for a very dull book.

Thus, I ask my readers' forgiveness for making certain alterations. For example, in the book, Elizabeth feel less than charitable at times towards her step mother in law Ann-Lucy. I am positive Elizabeth was, in reality, quite a wonderful lady and I have no proof whatsoever from any source at all that Elizabeth felt this way about Ann-Lucy. However, she had to have some foibles and failings, so please permit me to have invested her with a very small one —and one that is resolved by the end of the book.

The story line regarding the diplomatic mission to France that came to be known as the XYZ Affair is largely factual. However, it is my fabrication that Thomas Jefferson was behind both President Adams' initial attempt to keep the communiqués of this mission confidential, and his redaction of the French emissaries' names once the missives were published.

The plot line regarding the schism in the Braintrim Baptist Church, also factual, was quite problematical because extant details are very few. Although I consulted numerous sources both historical and primary, I was unable to uncover the names of the people involved in the land dispute that caused the schism, or the particulars of the dispute itself. This was a case of 'informed imagining' coming into play. Because there were land owners in this and other areas of Pennsylvania who had been granted land charters by both King George III and by William Penn (for the same tracts of land!), I extrapolated from that fact and chose to make that the underlying cause of the dispute.

Additionally, details such as the Réveillon dinner celebrated at the Sturdevants' home on Christmas Eve, dancing, card and game playing, and the consumption of wine, ale, and on occasion, spirits, while possibly at odds with some modern day sensibilities, would have been considered the norm in the late Colonial and early Regency period. They are included to lend the proper atmosphere and give an accurate representation of the time.

I hope my readers enjoy this next chapter in the story of Izzy and her remarkable life in the 18th—and now the early 19th century.

And I hope that, if you have not visited The Oldest House, where much of the action in this book takes place, that you will.


*~DLC*
*Doolittle Hill, 2015*

# A CHRISTMAS IN TIME

## CHAPTER ONE

"Are you warm enough?" Joshua Sturdevant asked his wife, Isabeau. Concern furrowed his brow as he leaned over from his window seat in the coach, and tucked the heavy woolen blanket more securely over her shoulders.

"I'm fine," she replied with a smile. "And the children are, too: sleeping, thank goodness!" she added with a glance at the seat beside her where their almost three year old son, Nicholas, snuggled with his baby sister Cordelia in a portable canvas and wood cradle-bed.

Joshua returned his wife's smile, and peered briefly out the curtained window of the private coach. He dropped the shade and re-fastened it almost immediately. "'Tis slowing, now, the snow," he said in a reassuring tone.

Isabeau, known to her husband and very close friends in their home town of Charlottesville, VA, as 'Izzy,' shot her husband a look. "You've been saying that since Tunkhannock," she chided him with another grin.

"But it truly is not snowing as much, now," Joshua insisted, with another quick peek outside. "The flakes are smaller, and fewer."

Izzy leaned her head back against the leather head cushion of the high seat and sighed. Her tall bonnet with the wide brim framed her face but it also kept her warm; never a 'hat person' in her former, modern existence in the twenty-first century, Izzy had found since taking up life in the late 1700's, that she was actually quite fond of headgear. Between the hat— velvet and leather—her fur-lined pelisse, her wool cloak, and the coach blanket, she was thoroughly comfortable despite the weather. The little brazier did its best to keep the worst of the chill out of the carriage's interior, but warm layers of clothing were also needed.

"I devoutly hope it were not folly we traveled," Joshua said, his voice low and urgent. "Making a fortnight's journey in the winter, with two babies..." he shook his head as he looked at his determined wife.

"We've not been back since our wedding," Izzy protested in a whisper. "Our children haven't met their aunt and uncle, or their grandfather, and we've not met John or Peter!" she finished insistently, mentioning Joshua's brother's children. "They and Nicholas are of an age, and can all play together," Izzy continued, clearly envisioning domestic bliss upon their arrival at Joshua's brother and sister in law's home in Braintrim. "And besides...we promised."

Elizabeth and Sam, in their many letters to Izzy and Josh since they had left Braintrim in June, 1796, had often asked when they would return to visit. The two women had become very close after Izzy's arrival at Braintrim. Elizabeth treasured the friendship she had built with Izzy in that year, and she considered her friend rather brilliant and very kind.

Although neither Elizabeth nor Sam was aware of the true facts behind Izzy's precipitous appearance at their house along the North Branch of the Susquehanna River in the late summer of 1795, they nonetheless both realized that Izzy was not typical. To Elizabeth in particular, this made their friendship all the more special, and Izzy's companionship had been much missed.

Elizabeth's letters had recounted many of the goings on in Braintrim Village as well as within the Sturdevant and Skinner families. Izzy was looking forward to meeting the children who had been born since she'd left, and reuniting with friends and extended family whom she had missed during her time away.

"Mmmm...'tis true. Sam and Elizabeth have written so much of the growth of the village, I will confess I am anxious to see it," Josh admitted, his dark blue eyes shining. "Two mills, of course, now, and many more and better shops I am told, and an hotel if you can imagine!"

Izzy gave a chuckle. "Well, whatever we see will be buried in snow!" she giggled as their private coach rolled on. It was an exaggeration, for although the storm itself was fierce, with considerable wind, only a couple of inches of snow in total had fallen. Izzy pointed to the front of the conveyance. "I hope Roger is all right," she murmured of their coachman.

"He be well, Madame, worry not," came the soft voice of Belinda Alleyne, the children's Nanny and Izzy's *de facto* lady's maid. Belinda's 'r' sounds were more like 'l' sounds, since in her native language of Island Carib, the two were pronounced the same, and her speech had a lilting pattern that was soothing to anyone listening. She sat on the bench seat opposite Izzy, alongside Joshua; boxes containing especially precious and fragile things occupied part of the space as well. "He have that box coat," Belinda added with a nod.

The 'box coat' was a heavy, hooded and caped creation meant to be worn by those driving coaches and carriages in the elements. Roger's was an extremely fine wool-lined hide coat, so it was water-repellant, and he wore several layers of warm clothes beneath, as well as knee high lined leather boots.

Roger Skerritt, the coachman, had come to work for the Sturdevants when they'd settled in Charlottesville. Referred by Josh's friend and mentor Thomas Jefferson, Roger had brought his niece, Belinda, with him when he'd interviewed, and both had been hired on the spot.

Slavery was the done thing in Charlottesville, but Izzy's modern sensibilities had not allowed her to keep slaves. Joshua, who had listened raptly as Izzy had explained that in the next century, slavery would be abolished in the United States, had taken his wife's side despite the fact that Jefferson was a slaveholder; he mostly kept quiet on the subject if it came up for discussion.

Izzy rarely gave glimpses into the future; indeed, she tried her best to not even think about what she knew would happen in the centuries to come. She insisted that to do so was unethical and also could be dangerous: such future knowledge could change their actions in the present, and thus change the future. So when she had spoken to Joshua about the abolition of slavery in the middle of the next century, he had known that the subject was of extreme importance, and had taken heed.

Roger, therefore, was a 'freedman' and Belinda a 'freedwoman' because as soon as Izzy and Josh purchased them, they filed the legal documents for manumission. Similar procedures would be followed for their cook, Mariah Celestin and their housemaid, Lucy Gumbs. All were West Indian by heritage, and from neighboring villages on the same coastal strip of the island of St. Vincent.

Luckily, they all spoke French and English in addition to their own indigenous Arawakan language. Izzy and Josh had made sure all their staff could also read and write English and French at least, and Izzy had been laughingly taught a little bit of rudimentary Island Carib in return.

Everyone got along well, forming a congenial family unit that lived quite harmoniously with the Sturdevants.

They were paid wages commensurate with what skilled laborers made, but the arrangement, though extremely satisfactory—and kept secret. Izzy and Joshua were going against the way things were done, and while they and their servants were more than content with the arrangement, they all realized that advertising it would be foolhardy.

When the Sturdevants had announced their intention to visit Joshua's brother and sister in law in Pennsylvania for the Christmas holidays, Mariah and Lucy had been tasked with the job of remaining in Charlottesville and giving the family home on Court Square a thorough cleaning while everyone else was away. Only too happy to escape what they perceived as the rigors of a long journey north to the untamed wilderness of rural Pennsylvania—and in the dead of winter, no less—the two women had been quite content to comply. They struggled with the winter time temperatures in Virginia, and imagined that any lands further north, like Pennsylvania, were little more than frozen tundra.

Of course, the Sturdevant home, a three story brick Federalist edifice, was their home, too, and Mariah and Lucy actually looked forward to the few weeks' time when they would have lovely dwelling all to themselves.

Now, Belinda snuggled more deeply into her own cloak, made of soft wool, just as fine, nearly, as her mistress', and the coach blanket that covered her from toes to chin, and wondered how much longer the trip would be. She had never seen snow before this journey, although ice had fallen, and hail, while she'd been in Charlottesville. The white stuff had beguiled her so much that she had written back to Mariah and Lucy of the amazing phenomenon.

"Can you tell where we are?" Izzy asked her husband a while later.

Josh obligingly peered out of the coach window again. It was late afternoon now, and although the snowfall made everything seem bright, an indigo and crimson blush in the western sky told Josh that the sun had already set. The good news was, the sunset meant that the weather was finally clearing.

"We are very near Black Walnut Bottom," he answered, also giving his meteorological observations.

"Only a few more miles!" Izzy crowed happily. At the speed the coach was able to make over the snow-covered dirt road, that meant about an hour.

## CHAPTER TWO

"Oh, you are here, you are here, you are finally here!" exulted Elizabeth, flinging her arms wide to hug her dear friend and sister in law. She wore a high waisted dress in navy and tan plaid wool, a creamy fichu filling in the low cut neckline. An ivory wool shawl with elaborate patterning and fringe accessorized the dress. As she drew back to look at Izzy, Elizabeth's blue eyes sparkled in her slender face, and two pearl ear bobs peeked from under her soft blonde hair and lacy cap.

The wood-planked front door had swung open just moments before to reveal the long awaited visitors just alighting from their coach on the snow-covered flagstone terrace that filled the space between the Susquehanna River and the front of the Sam Sturdevants' home.

Izzy hugged Elizabeth back with much happiness: not only to be, at last, at their house, but to have completed the long journey safely.

Although the three story black walnut sided home by the river was Elizabeth's and Sam's residence, Izzy considered it hers in a way, as well. What only Izzy and Josh knew was that Izzy had been acquainted with that same dwelling in her own, twenty-first century time. Called 'The Oldest House' because it had been built in 1781 and was still standing as the oldest frame dwelling in four surrounding counties, the home had been run in modern times as a living museum, by the Oldest House Historical Society in what had become Laceyville, PA.

Izzy had worked as a volunteer tour guide and display coordinator at the House, and so had developed a deep affection for it. Once she had stumbled through that time portal one hot August afternoon and found herself in the past—which was the House's past, too—the rooms and halls she had come to know so well in her own time were welcome, familiar things, even if much of the eighteenth century world was not. And, of course, the House was where Izzy had met Josh.

For all these reasons, the House was much beloved by Izzy, who now gave Elizabeth a last hug and stepped inside, looking around at the ground floor Keeping Room in which she found herself, and smiling.

Like the 'Great Rooms' fashionable in Izzy's own time, the Colonial and post-Colonial 'Keeping Room' was where much of the family's life was conducted. Some cooking, baking, spinning and so on were done here. Children had lessons here and played here. Foodstuffs were stored here and in the summer, because it was cool, families sometimes slept here. Conversely, in winter, the Keeping Room was always warm, and so sometimes families would spend the night before the fire rather than brave the chilly bedchambers or dormitories upstairs.

Now, the Oldest House's Keeping Room was welcomingly bright and cozy. White pine branches from the nearby woods and hand dipped candles tied with red and green ribbon decorated each of the room's windows, and more pine boughs were draped across the huge black walnut mantel of the front fireplace. Sprigs of holly, bright with crimson berries, occupied a large earthenware vase on a sideboard. A large ball of mistletoe tied with more green and red ribbon hung suspended from one of the hand hewn rafters overhead. Oil lamps glowed from the rustic wooden table, and a bowl of apples there perfumed the air, as did the flames crackling merrily in the fireplace, and whatever hung simmering on the iron swing arm nearby.

A large spinning wheel in one corner held skeins of creamy wool on their way to being yarn, and along the fieldstone walls were earthenware crocks and tightly woven baskets containing all manner of grains and root vegetables. Shelves along the other side of the Keeping Room held row upon row of pickled vegetables and preserved fruit in various sized crocks that shone a deep chocolate brown, and colorful hand stitched quilts draped and decorated the wooden chairs throughout.

Tibbsy, the Sturdevants' black and white cat, also decorated a chair, curled up atop a few burlap sacks, nose in his tail, apparently asleep, but with one eye slitted to spot movement by any vermin who dared enter his domain. Tibbsy was a superb mouser, and Martha—the Sturdevants' cook and housekeeper—rarely had problems with rodents getting into the food.

Overhead, hand-hewn beams held a variety of cook pots and household equipment, along with drying herbs, long strings of dried beans and stone fruits, and fat ristras of bronze onions and deep red peppers.

Izzy knew that the cold larder in the northwest corner of the house kept all manner of salted and cured meats and fish as well as eggs, milk and some fresh items that needed to be kept chilled. Next to it, on the western side, the root cellar was where gourds, tubers and the like were warehoused to see the family through until spring.

Both spaces had been dug into the bank of earth up against which the house was built and, along with insulating straw, kept things quite cool. Ice, gathered in winter, helped the process and Izzy had been surprised to learn that ice from March might still be hard and cold the following August, if insulated properly.

Something delicious was cooking, no doubt keeping warm in the rear of the double fireplace, and Izzy's mouth watered. It had been a very long journey, and their mid day snack of bread, cheese and ale at the Red Lion Tavern in Tunkhannock, when they had also changed to their final team of horses, had been a very long time ago.

Sam, Josh's brother and Elizabeth's husband, clattered down the stairs into the Keeping Room at this juncture, and swept his twin up in a bear hug. Then he gave Izzy a slightly more delicate embrace of welcome, and beamed at them.

"You have arrived!" he announced as though he didn't quite believe his eyes. Sam wore the traditional brown knee breeches, light hose, and black buckled shoes with a full-cut ivory shirt, neck cloth, and an embroidered dark brown leather vest beneath a charcoal colored wool jacket. His hair, the same raven black as Josh's, was tied back in a small queue, and his sky blue eyes were merry.

"Aye, we have, brother," Josh confirmed, his grin nearly as huge as his brother's.

"And is this young Nicholas, then?" Sam asked, looking at the just awakened toddler clinging fiercely to his father's neck and looking around him in bewilderment.

"Aye, 'tis he," Josh replied, and made introductions.

Martha had bustled forward to take Josh's great-coat and Izzy's cloak and pelisse, and Sam now eyed his twin's long 'pantaloon' trousers with curiosity. Paired with a navy frock coat, embroidered vest, shirt and stock, the trousers gave Josh's slim build an elegant line that his brother could not help but remark on.

"Aye, 'tis the coming fashion in Europe and England," Josh told Sam with a grin. "And Mr. Jefferson wears them almost exclusively now, saying they are sober and restrained: the right clothing for the rational man," Josh explained.

Sam merely raised his eyebrows and noted that the style was a good looking one, if strange to the eye of someone who was used to men in breeches and hose.

Meanwhile, Elizabeth was exclaiming over Cordelia, who slept in her mother's arms, not bothered in the least by the dismount from the coach, the enthusiastic hugging, or all the exclamations and chatter.

"She is an angel," Elizabeth breathed, her brown eyes shining. "Oh, I should so like to have a daughter," she added hopefully.

Izzy smiled, and then Sam had to have a turn admiring Cordelia while Elizabeth met her nephew.

"I'm so happy to see you looking so well," Izzy told Elizabeth, giving her another long look.

"And you!" Elizabeth returned. She reached out and felt the cuff of Izzy's empire-waisted, long-sleeved woven jacquard dress in a deep mulberry wool. "So very soft," she murmured.

"There is an excellent draper's shop very near us," Izzy explained, "who has the most wonderful woolens and silks, especially." She tucked a couple of wayward russet curls back under her embroidered cap as she spoke, hoping she didn't look too disheveled after the long journey.

A young girl, Becky, with skin the color of caramel, brought two little boys downstairs a moment later: John and Peter, the Samuel Sturdevants' two young sons. Becky was the younger sister of Martha, and had assumed the function of nanny and housemaid once Elizabeth and Sam's first son had been born. Martha's son—she was a widow, her husband having been killed in the Revolutionary War—Ephraim was now in his teens, and worked alongside his mother and aunt in keeping the Sturdevant home running smoothly. He was also currently apprenticed at one of Sam's sawmills.

"I can't believe I am meeting you at last!" Izzy told her nephews. John, who was three and a half and looked like a small version of his father, shook his aunt's hand solemnly while Peter, who wasn't quite two, gazed placidly from Becky's arms at the stranger with round blue eyes that were his mother's.

While these introductions were being made, Martha welcomed Roger and Belinda and took care of the luggage that had been fastened to the rear of the coach. Then everyone settled down at the long wooden table, and Martha poured fragrant mulled cider into little pewter cups and passed them around.

Sam raised his cup to make a toast, but Joshua stayed his hand.

"I am afraid, brother, we bring with us sad news out of Virginia," Josh announced solemnly. "I do not think you will have heard, yet, as the news met us while we were traveling through New York," he began, looking at his wife as though for confirmation.

Izzy nodded.

Elizabeth looked worried.

Sam frowned.

"President Washington has died," Joshua said. "So, let our first toast be to him, his achievements in freeing this great country, and for guiding its nascent steps as its first President."

## CHAPTER THREE

The news of Washington's death lent an air of solemnity to the reunion dinner that evening, but everyone's joy at being together once more did not remain shadowed for long. Over the warm, spiced cider, Josh and Izzy shared what they knew about the death of the President, which they had learned of in Philadelphia.

"He died on the fourteenth," Izzy began, "and there was a very private service four days later at Mount Vernon," she added.

"What struck him down?" Elizabeth asked, frowning so that a thin line appeared between her gentle brows.

"They say he took a chill and his throat became inflamed," Josh answered solemnly.

"And none could cure it?" Sam asked, surprised. "I should imagine the President would have had the best doctors..."

"Aye, he did," Josh agreed with a look from under his brows at Izzy. "But they had no medicine that was able to quell the inflammation."

Izzy said nothing. She had told Josh that from what she had heard, Washington's terminal illness had almost certainly been what medicine in her own day would have diagnosed as epiglottitis. While streptococcus was likely involved, even without penicillin—which wouldn't be discovered for around a century—the President could have possibly been saved with intubation. However, that was a medical technique not known in 1799, though its cousin, tracheotomy, was. However, tracheotomies often resulted in sepsis and the death of the patient, anyway.

"So he—..." Elizabeth could not say the words.

"He could not breathe, and became unconscious," Joshua put in quickly. "And then he died."

It had been a frightening and unpleasant death according to the eyewitness accounts that had begun to circulate. But this was neither the time or the place, or the audience, to discuss that in detail. "We would have attended, had we not already been on our way here," Josh continued, shifting the subject somewhat. He and Izzy and the children had left Charlottesville on December seventh; now, it was the twenty-third, and Josh felt that in spite of the inclement weather during the most recent two days, they had made excellent time on the journey.

Part of the reason for their good time had been that although the coach belonged to them, they had hired fresh teams of horses at frequent and convenient intervals throughout the journey. This had meant they had traveled as swiftly as possible. In addition, they had used the King's Highway for a part of the journey: although it was unpaved—paving being a wonder of Izzy's time that had yet to be created in 1799—it was so well traveled its surface was hard packed and quite smooth.

When Josh had lamented privately to his wife of the time and trouble of travel in his era and confessed that he feared she would be most impatient with their progress, Izzy had just laughed and said that she thought their journey an adventure.

Leading from Charleston to Boston, the King's Highway was the route taken by the U.S. Mail, and as such it was also well served with inns, taverns and towns that had sprung up along it. Izzy had insisted on creating 'sandwiches' for their little traveling party, not unlike the one she had made the summer she'd arrived at the Sturdevant home, to the surprise and delight of everyone. These quick but filling meals meant that they did not have to stop to have a sit-down dinner each day, but could eat as they went, pausing only to change teams of horses, and on occasion, staying the night at an inn or tavern along the way, where Izzy could purchase any needed items and replenish her sandwich stock for the next couple of days.

The word 'picnic' was new to the English language, being of French origin—'pique-nique'—but picnicking was exactly what the Joshua Sturdevant family did, along with their servants, on the road from Charlottesville to Braintrim.

Once they had passed Philadelphia, they had traveled the Northwest Territory Route which would become the Turnpike and Route 6 in Izzy's time. There, they had seen snow on the ground in the highest elevations, but had not encountered the foul weather itself until the last days of their journey.

"I understand that many of Washington's Masonic brethren served as pallbearers," Izzy said now as Martha, noting her cup was empty, re-filled it.

"And the military was well represented, too, of course," Josh amended. "We heard in Philadelphia that they will hold the official funeral there the day after Christmas."

Sam nodded. "As the nation's capital, they should," he agreed.

"Oh, but Washington, D.C. is nearly complete!" Elizabeth exclaimed. "It must be so exciting, to be nearby and watch it come to life," she added, her eyes sparkling.

"I love L'Enfant's design," Izzy admitted. "And the parks and wide boulevards are lovely."

Joshua smiled. "It is a very beautiful city, fitting to be our nation's capital. But I wonder if it will be ready in time?" he queried.

At Sam's and Elizabeth's curious looks, he elaborated. They all knew that the temperamental L'Enfant had been fired by the late President Washington just a year or so after his designs had been accepted. The surveying and final planning for the nation's new capital was being done by Andrew Ellicott and Benjamin Banneker. Both men had been part of L'Enfant's original team, and once the testy architect departed, they had been able to reproduce the layout of L'Enfant's Washington down to the last street, park and building.

Meanwhile, of course, Congress had designated Philadelphia as the nation's capital for only ten years: the time would be up in 1800, so Washington, D.C. had to be ready.

Martha gave the signal to Elizabeth that supper was ready, and they all mounted the stairs to the first floor dining room and the large cherry wood table that Izzy knew so well.

40

## CHAPTER FOUR

Over supper, Sam and Elizabeth asked many questions about the young city of Charlottesville, Virginia, where Izzy and Josh had settled. Like Washington, Charlottesville was set out on a grid, with parks and other amenities gracing the layout.

"Our house is really quite perfectly situated," Izzy explained, repeating what she had detailed in her many letters to Elizabeth and Sam.

She described the newly-built three story wood and brick home in great detail, and Elizabeth and Sam listened avidly, even though they had read much the same in Izzy's letters.

"We are directly on Courthouse Square, which is on the north end of the city. The courthouse itself, where of course Josh conducts a great deal of his business, is just a short distance from our front door."

"And although Izzy has her own gig and could certainly go down to Three Notch'd Road," Joshua began proudly, referencing the main street in Charlottesville, "many shops have opened and are thriving around our square."

At the mention of 'her own gig,' Elizabeth caught her smiling lips in her teeth and gave her sister in law a delighted look, her eyebrows raised and her eyes round. "And do you go to the Capitol as well?" she asked, slightly breathless.

"'Tis a day's journey each way," Josh explained. "We have gone, and we shall again, but my work requires that I only be there every several weeks," he explained.

"In your letters, you mention Monticello a great deal," offered Sam, leadingly.

"Oh, yes, Monticello's only three miles away from us," Izzy chimed in with enthusiasm. "I can walk it on a fine day, and I have, although if I take the children I drive the gig," she added with a smile.

"Mr. Jefferson enjoys having the children visit?" Elizabeth asked, sounding disbelieving.

Izzy nodded. "He does. I generally confine them to the gardens, and then we all have tea—they have lemon barley water, for Monticello has a potable well —on the veranda. But Josh visits often for work, and at least once a fortnight, we go to dinner there," she added. As she spoke, she realized anew just how remarkable it was that she and Josh were among the great Thomas Jefferson's closest friends.

"Your description of the dining room there was wonderful," Elizabeth noted. Jefferson's dining room at Monticello featured huge windows that allowed the guests to feel as though they were dining out of doors; the Vice President's cuisine was also famous for being delectably influenced by French tastes, and Izzy had especially enjoyed it.

"But tell us more about Charlottesville," urged Sam as he ate.

"There's a wonderful tailor, a jeweler, a gunsmith and a print shop," Izzy told him. "And a second milliner just opened up as well, next to the draper, although the general store downtown has a larger selection," she mused. "But we do have very high quality items in our smaller stores on the square," she admitted.

"To the east, on the Rivanna River, there are two mills as well, brother," Josh told Sam, knowing of his interests. "A sawmill and a grist mill. There is talk, too, of some kind of textile mill being located there, but I am not sure of the details."

"A man named Slater has a thriving yarn spinning mill in Pawtucket, Rhode Island," offered Sam thoughtfully. "And Mr. Whitney's sawtoothed cotton ginning machine has made the creation of cotton fabric far more efficient." He took a sip of the ale he drank with dinner, and sighed. "There are several other textile mills springing up along rivers in Massachusetts," he noted, sounding a bit envious. "Mayhap the textile industry will also come to Braintrim!" he declared hopefully. "We have two good streams and the Susquehanna," he added with a smile.

"What I like about Charlottesville is that, even though it is a city, it's more like a small town, really," Izzy put in.

"I think that is because there is no navigable river there," Sam replied analytically. "Goods and so forth come upriver and then overland to Charlottesville—would it be the James River, to Richmond?" he asked his twin.

Josh nodded. "Or sometimes via the Rappahannock, but the overland journey is very hard from there, as there are no good roads. And 'tis true, the Rivanna is quite small. Good for pleasure craft, but not for trade ships of any size."

"But that keeps Charlottesville small," Sam noted. "Which is not a bad thing. Here, however, the Susquehanna River means that Braintrim Village has riverboat access, and of course the creeks flowing into the river mean millworks, and that brings yet more people here both to do business and to live."

"What of the ferry boat you talked of in your letters recently?" Josh inquired with a grin. His brother was nothing if not an astute and enterprising businessman, and had spoken of trying to set up a cross-river service near the village of Braintrim.

Sam shook his head. "We have not found the right person, yet, though I have an idea…and I do believe we have discovered a navigable spot where the river is both calm and not so wide as may be elsewhere," he explained.

"Well, perhaps soon," Izzy put in encouragingly. The first ferry would in fact serve Braintrim and the southern shore of the Susquehanna River just two years hence.

"And is your church on the square, as well as all the shops you speak of?" Sam asked. As the son of the Baptist minister who had founded the Braintrim Baptist Church, he was naturally interested.

"Sadly, there is no church building yet," Josh replied, shaking his head. "Though there is a thriving worship community. We use the courthouse."

# CHAPTER FIVE

Supper was a bit later than usual because it had been delayed until Josh and Izzy's arrival. However, it was a splendid repast, and Martha presented three hearty and tempting courses—one more than the usual two. Additionally, Sam poured out his best claret for the ladies while he and his twin enjoyed some of the area's finest ale.

The first course was a hot, creamy root vegetable soup consisting of puréed turnips, swedes, and potatoes enlivened by herbs and precious salt. With it, Martha served an assortment of pickled vegetables and freshly baked biscuits. Izzy remembered how delicious Martha's cooking was from the last time she'd been at her in laws', and was happy to see that her skills had, if anything, increased.

The second course saw a variety of smoked fish and meats as well as a game pie spiced with thyme and sage, and studded with dried blueberries. Izzy wasn't sure what sort of game was in the pie and didn't have a chance to inquire, as conversation was so lively around the expansion of Braintrim, but she suspected quail and possibly pheasant. Both birds, she knew, were plentiful in the area's dense forests, woodlands and meadows.

Dessert arrived in the form of a rich custard tart, preserved red cherries that glistened in their small bowl, dried figs, nuts, and a spice cake.

It was such a pleasure to be at rest, finally, and in one place that Izzy—as well as Josh, she noticed—ate some of everything, cleaned her plate and drained her glass. Josh didn't smoke, but Sam still did, so the two of them adjourned after dinner to the Keeping Room, where Sam would light his long clay pipe and the two of them could discuss politics, and business, and whatever else took their fancy.

Izzy and Elizabeth, meanwhile, repaired to the top floor of the house where Nicholas, Cordelia, John and Peter all awaited them. There were three dedicated bedchambers here on the top floor: one for Sam and Elizabeth and two for 'guests.' Izzy had stayed in one of these when she had first arrived in 1795, and was pleased to see her trunks along with Josh's in that room once again.

The rest of the upstairs was what Izzy called 'open plan,' and when the children were older, they would very likely sleep here rather than in their parents' room as they did now. Also, travelers coming upriver who broke their journey at the house had, in the past, been given lodging in this space. However, with the growth of Braintrim Village and the establishment now of the village's first hotel, this upstairs space was not often needed by passing travelers, and had become the *de facto* nursery and Elizabeth's personal sitting room.

It was to a comfortable chair and small settee that Izzy and Elizabeth went now, and prepared to tend to their children.

Peter was still nursing, but John had eaten a 'nursery version' of what the adults had had for dinner, and was amusing himself now, sitting on the floor and playing with a wooden puzzle his father had carved for him. Nicholas had also eaten the nursery dinner, and watched John now, entranced by his older cousin's toy.

"He is weaned, then?" Elizabeth asked Izzy of Nicholas.

"Yes," Izzy replied with a grin as Cordelia latched on and began to suck vigorously. "But sometimes he'll still want to nurse, after Cordy's finished," she laughed. "Since his baby teeth are in, it can be a bit uncomfortable," she admitted, and made a face that caused Elizabeth to laugh.

"After we had John, I was not certain we would have another, since the getting of him had not been easy," Elizabeth said, low, while her younger son Peter nursed quietly.

Izzy remembered: Elizabeth had told her that it had taken several months for her to fall pregnant, and that when she had, she'd needed to be quite careful until the baby was full term. Izzy and Josh had timed their wedding so that Izzy could assist at Elizabeth's lying-in, and although her midwifery skills had been scant, Izzy's knowledge of modern medicine had helped a great deal in the delivery.

"But I was yet nursing John when I discovered I was carrying Peter," Elizabeth revealed, her pale face blushing at the intimacy of the conversation. She reveled in it, however: Izzy had been her first girlfriend as a married woman, and was still her closest. Now that they were related by marriage, Elizabeth felt there was very little she could not speak about with Izzy, and Izzy felt the same.

The distance between them that had occurred when Izzy moved away with Josh had disappeared almost immediately upon the two women's reunion earlier that evening, and of course, the frequent letters the two had exchanged—nearly twice a week sometimes—had kept the relationship robust.

Izzy smiled, and shifted her daughter slightly.

"But it did not take you long at all!" Elizabeth continued, envious. "Was it that tea you got from Mrs. Charney?" she asked, mentioning an herbalist out near Wyalusing that Izzy had visited.

Izzy shrugged. "Maybe. But you took it, too, didn't you?" she asked, and Elizabeth nodded.

"Aye, but I fear had I not, I might never have had a child at all."

"And two boys," Izzy crowed. "Sam must be over the moon!"

"That he is. But I so would like a daughter," Elizabeth said again, with a longing gaze at Cordelia.

Izzy smiled. Before she'd decided to remain in the past with Josh, she'd returned to her own time to prepare, and had researched him and his family. Although she tried now to keep what she knew in the back recesses of her mind, she was aware of facts about the future of the Sturdevant family.

She knew, for example, that Elizabeth would have at least two daughters: Clarissa in 1802 and Eunice the year after. What she did not know was whether either girl lived to adulthood, as genealogical records on them had not been complete.

It was this 'future knowledge' that Izzy found sometimes troublesome: she rarely tripped up and said anything too revealing, but on occasion the temptation to alter what she knew would be a less than positive outcome was strong. In these moments, she tried to bite her tongue and sit on her hands and hum 'Turn, Turn, Turn' by the Byrds until the temptation passed.

Now, the children had been fed, and it was time to settle them down for the night. John slept on a low trundle bed that pulled out from underneath his parents' 'cannonball' four poster, while Peter was in a large cradle next to him.

At home in Charlottesville, Nicholas had a similar accommodation, and Cordelia had her own cradle, too, although they were in their nursery, not in their parents' bedchamber.

Here, however, Izzy had been unsure what sort of arrangement would be made. She was pleased to see that Sam had fixed up a small child's pallet in a corner of the guest room Izzy and Josh would occupy. That bed would be for Nicholas, while Cordelia would sleep in a small cradle that Sam had made for one of his own future children.

## CHAPTER SIX

With Becky and Belinda watching over their respective charges as they fell asleep, Elizabeth and Izzy made their way down to the Keeping Room and found their husbands deep in conversation. The men looked up, and their solemn faces lighted when they saw their wives.

"I have been filling Sam in on the goings on in France," Josh said as Izzy sat next to him in a comfy cane-seated chair with a gracefully turned spindle back that matched his own.

Elizabeth positioned herself in a similar chair that her husband had vacated, and motioned for her to take. Sam moved to the center of a long bench that was placed perpendicularly to the large fireplace, and re-lit his pipe.

Izzy shot Josh a look. "You have?" she asked.

"Well, the outline of the matter," Josh amended quickly.

"Oh, I do very much wish to hear all about that," Elizabeth said, retrieving a needlework project from a basket to one side of the fireplace. "But I feel there is so much I want to hear about—and Sam does, too," she added, encompassing her husband in her lively look.

"Aye. Your letters have been the subject of many long discussions in this house," Sam noted with a grin. "But there is truly nothing like hearing it in person, and having a chance to ask questions as they come to mind," he added.

"So—let me see," Elizabeth mused, looking around delightedly at everyone. "How was your honeymoon trip to England?"

Izzy and Josh had visited England following their wedding, and although Izzy's long letters had extensively described nearly every moment of their trip, she and Josh gladly recapped the highlights now for their family.

Although they had originally thought to visit what would be Italy in Izzy's day, unrest on the continent and the continuing efforts by Napoleon Bonaparte to conquer more and more of Europe had persuaded Izzy and Josh to confine their honeymoon abroad to England.

They had travelled first by boat to Southampton, then gone overland by coach to London, stopping on the way at the home of friends of Reverend Samuel's grandfather, George and Cassandra Austen.

The surname had been familiar to Izzy, but she had assumed it to be a common enough one, until they had arrived and been introduced to the Reverend George, his wife, and their children: James, Henry, Francis, Charles, Cassandra and Jane. It was then that Izzy realized whose home they were stopping at, and whom they were really meeting.

It had been all she could do to keep the knowledge to herself, but she took every opportunity to watch the Austens' younger daughter, and even converse with her when the opportunity arose.

All of the Austens' children had come to meet the American visitors, and brought their own families, for the Austens' children were by then quite grown up. Only the two daughters, yet unmarried, still lived at home. The first night the Austens held a large family dinner at which Izzy and Josh were their honored guests.

On the second night of their visit, the Reverend George had urged his daughters to entertain their visitors after the evening meal. Cassandra had played the pianoforte, performing a number of tunes that Izzy had known because they were still popular in her own time.

Izzy had complimented the Austens on their artistic daughter, then, for Cassandra also did landscapes in watercolors, some of which were quite pretty.

That same evening, after her sister had played, Jane had been persuaded to give a reading of some of her latest work.

'She writes stories,' Mrs. Austen had explained, thinking quite naturally that Izzy and Josh would not know this,'and we do so enjoy hearing them.'

Izzy had nodded and murmured that the gift of being able to write good fiction was truly one to be appreciated, and had turned to listen to the young woman.

Jane Austen was at that time in the summer of 1795, twenty years old. A small, slight woman with brown hair and a rather ordinary face that was enlivened on occasion by strong emotion, her greatest beauty was a pair of fine, large brown eyes. These brimmed with intelligence and wit and in the few short conversations Izzy had enjoyed with the future author, Jane's wry sense of humor had made itself deliciously apparent.

She thought that Jane had enjoyed talking to her, too. Izzy maintained her assumed persona as an escaped French noblewoman, but her point of view and way of expressing herself were distinctly different, even given her eighteenth century identity.

As they had walked in the garden or chatted in the sitting room, Jane had appeared quite intrigued with her family's American visitor, joining eagerly in discussions of topics ranging from politics to social mores to music to sewing, at which she excelled. Izzy thought that her own inabilities in this area were a source of much amusement to Jane.

The two women appeared to have several opinions in common; the fact that these opinions, particularly concerning women, society and marriage, were considered 'radical' at the time, only served to make Izzy and Jane grow more fond of each other.

Izzy would ask, as they took their leave the following day, if she might write to Jane and so continue their exchange of ideas, and Jane had agreed readily and promised to reply. In the ensuing three years, missives would cross back and forth across the Atlantic, detailing Izzy's new life in Charlottesville with descriptions of the people she met, and Jane's life in England including her trips to Bath, and her developing attitudes towards it.

Now on this second evening at the Austens', the fragment of story that Jane had read had been part of a tale of two sisters, Elinor and Marianne, and had been told in epistolary form. The letter writing format wasn't one of Izzy's favorites, but she had found herself not caring as she'd listened raptly to what certainly was an early draft of what would become Jane Austen's *Sense and Sensibility*. It had been all she could do just to keep her jaw off the floor!

From Hampshire, Josh and Izzy had made a side excursion to Stonehenge and then traveled to London, where they had spent several days. Josh had

had letters of introduction from Jefferson and other men of note in the U.S., and so they had been wined and dined in 'The City' by barristers, statesmen, Lords and Members of Parliament.

The Prime Minister, William Pitt the Younger, had a fair amount of support from both Whigs and Tories, since Great Britain was still at war with France, and had been since 1792. A general election shortly before Izzy and Josh's arrival had not changed much of the political landscape.

England, along with various allies that formed 'coalitions' throughout this period, sought overall to stanch the spread of French—actually Napoleonic— influence in Europe, the Middle East and Northern Africa.

The unrest meant that both the French and the English—at the time, the two major Western world powers— 'courted' the new country of the United States in efforts to gain an important ally. At the time of Josh and Izzy's honeymoon, the bankrupting of France by the Napoleonic Wars and 'the Little General's' eventual defeat were both still in the future.

However, during one remarkable 'salon' in London where both men and women talked politics as they drank sherry or port, Izzy had suggested that the cost of Napoleon's ego-driven invasions would eventually take its toll.

' 'Tis why they began raiding your merchant ships,' Pitt had commented to her laconically. ' 'Tis the quickest and I daresay the most easy way to raise fresh cash.' Pitt had paused. 'And of course, there is also land,' he had added.

Izzy had nodded and smiled. 'Indeed, Prime Minister: France controls a great tract of land in the center and West of the continent of which the United States occupies the Eastern portion,' she had noted. 'Mayhap they will be so hard pressed for cash that they will sell their interests in the New World to us,' she had murmured.

No one had called this idea foolish, and Izzy had privately wondered if the assembled party would recall this conversation in a few years once the 'Louisiana Purchase' was achieved in 1803.

Izzy had also taken the opportunity of being in London to do some serious shopping. Izzy knew the most stylish togs would be found at the many couturiers and milliners in London. She'd ordered several new day dresses and a few evening gowns as well as a pelisse, petticoats, hats, hair ornaments, shoes, fans, gloves and reticules, the last of which were just coming into their own as an accessory.

Fortunately, the gold she'd brought back from her own time had made Izzy a wealthy woman. Once Josh began working as an attorney and Jefferson's aide upon their return to the States, his salary would increase their overall worth as well. So Izzy was comfortable spending some money on new and up to date fashion, as well as on gifts to bring or send back to friends and family.

After their time in London, they had gone to the heart of the country, the picturesque villages that would be much unchanged even in Izzy's own time. They'd also visited Oxford and Cambridge, and gone up to York where they'd been received by Frederick Howard, the Fifth Earl of Carlisle at Castle Howard, a stately home Izzy had visited in modern times. The Earl was another old friend of Josh's great grandfather.

Carlisle's extensive collection of paintings had fascinated Izzy: most were from the Orléans Collection and had been the property of the Duke of Orléans prior to the French Revolution. Izzy's assumed persona as a French Countess who had fled the Revolution in France had delighted the Earl, who took great pleasure in bowing to Izzy, and receiving her answering curtsey, whenever they encountered each other.

The stately home was as stunning and beautiful as it had been in Izzy's own day, as were the grounds and gardens. Luckily, they had fine weather while they were in York, as well, and a chance to visit the walled city itself, one of the oldest in the country.

The Earl's ward, eight year old George Gordon Byron, Sixth Baron Byron, had been in residence at Castle Howard during their visit as well, and Izzy had once again bitten her lip and said nothing when she'd met the child who would become one of the most highly regarded English poets of all time.

Then Izzy and Josh had gone West to Liverpool, where they'd boarded a ship to make their return journey across the Atlantic, and back to their new home in Charlottesville.

"We arrived just in time to help Mr. Jefferson work on his campaign," Josh revealed now to his twin and Elizabeth. "Although he lost."

Izzy nodded. "Yes, but he will stand for President next year, against Mr. Adams," she put in.

"And do you think he will win?" Sam asked, giving his sister in law a keen look.

Izzy bit her lip, but nodded cautiously. "I do think he may, yes," she admitted with a grin.

## CHAPTER SEVEN

The following day, of course, was Christmas Eve Day, and in the Keeping Room, preparations were underway for that evening's activities and those of the holiday itself. Although Izzy did not know it, months before when Elizabeth and Sam had learned that Izzy and Josh would be with them for Christmas they had asked acquaintances of theirs from upriver about French Christmas customs.

'I should like to make a special effort for Madame Sturdevant,' Elizabeth had told Noiret and Annaliese Charrette; the couple had remembered 'Isabeau de Villehardouin' from 1795 since they had been the ones coordinating Izzy's presumed move to the settlement at Azilum. That settlement had been prepared for the arrival of Marie Antoinette and her children, but she and the Dauphin and Dauphine were guillotined before that could happen.

Once Izzy had fallen in love with Josh, of course, she had not left the Sturdevant home.

The Charrettes had been only too glad to share a few of the typical French customs with Elizabeth, and so she and Martha had been planning a version of the French Christmas Eve 'Réveillon' for some time.

Now, the schedule was to attend the usual Christmas Eve service at the Baptist Church in the village where the Reverend Samuel Sturdevant would preach. Then they would return to the house and enjoy what Elizabeth was calling to herself a 'New World Réveillon.' It would not be, perhaps, as festive as the traditional French version, but she hoped it would please Izzy.

In Braintrim at that time, although there were other denominations, many people, including the Sturdevants, were Baptists. The Reverend Samuel Sturdevant still led the growing flock of the faithful at the church he founded in the village; Izzy knew that two-hundred -plus years on, that church would still have a thriving, welcoming congregation. Reverend Sturdevant's late wife, Sarah, had been a Methodist, and the Reverend thought highly of that denomination as well.

For Baptists in particular, as well as Lutherans and some others, the period of Advent leading up to Christmas was far more solemn that it would be in Izzy's own time. Christmas itself, while joyous, was overall a quieter celebration too. It would not be until the mid to late 1800's that German traditions such as the 'Christmas Tree' would be adopted in the English-speaking world, and not until the late 1800's that the holiday became more secular than spiritual.

Because Izzy had introduced herself as 'Isabeau de Villehardouin, Comtesse de Billy' when she had arrived at the Sturdevants' home in 1795, everyone had taken her for a member of the French nobility.

Although Izzy's religion had never been discussed, the Sturdevants had assumed her to be a 'Papist,' or Catholic, since members of the French nobility generally were.

Yet they had included her in their daily prayers and also in their twice-weekly church services. When she'd married Josh, she had become a *de facto* Baptist, although once the couple had moved to Charlottesville and become close associates of Jefferson, their point of view as well as their practice, changed.

Jefferson had been raised an Anglican, or Episcopalian as it would come to be called in the United States. Yet he had been much influenced by the Enlightenment, so that by the time Izzy and Josh knew him, he was more of a Deist and did not align himself with any particular sect.

Since the church services in Charlottesville leaned heavily towards the Anglican—the first church there would be Christ Episcopal, built in 1820 —and since the others in Charlottesville society with whom Josh and Izzy associated were Anglican, they thought of themselves as belonging to that denomination more than any other.

However, back home in Braintrim, Josh and Izzy reverted to the family's traditional Baptist traditions and indeed, did not find it so very different —not in that time, at any rate.

So Christmas Eve and Christmas Day were centered around church and family, visiting, and reverently celebratory feasting. In the interval between Christmas and New Year's, holiday visits to neighbors and friends would be made, and Elizabeth had excitedly told Izzy that a gala ball was scheduled as well.

"I do hope you brought a gown?" Elizabeth inquired Christmas Eve morning after breakfast. They were seated in the River Room, as Izzy called it, whose strong, clear light from the many windows made Elizabeth favor it for sewing and other close work. She had one of her sons' small smocks in hand now, and was embroidering it. She wore a day dress of soft dark blue wool with a snowy fichu and cap.

"I did," Izzy replied with a smile. She had opted for a day dress in a black and white striped calico, and a strip of lace tied around her upswept red hair in lieu of a cap. She was wrapping some mysterious boxes and oddly shaped packages with various bits of brightly colored ribbon. "Will the ball be at the Hall behind your father's tavern?" she asked, recalling the dance she'd gone to there her very first week back in 1795. She always remembered it as the evening she had fallen in love with Joshua.

Elizabeth smiled back. "Yes indeed!" she confirmed.

Although gifts were given at Christmas, they were generally small, useful presents given from masters or heads of households to their servants or slaves; it was unusual for equals to exchange gifts, although among family members it was becoming more common.

However, because it had been three years since Josh and Izzy had been 'home' with Sam and Elizabeth, and because they had travelled, and now lived in a more sophisticated town, they had brought a number of items to give to their in laws. It was some of these that Izzy wrapped now.

Elizabeth and Sam had also prepared gifts to give to Izzy and Josh, and Elizabeth had decided that the exchange would take place late Christmas Day after the Skinners and Reverend Sturdevant and his family had joined them for Christmas Dinner.

"Father in law is re-married," Elizabeth reminded Izzy now, who nodded.

"Yes, just shortly after Josh and I wed, if I recall aright," Izzy confirmed.

"Mmmm…she had five children from her marriage to Mr. Cooley, and I wrote to say that two years ago she had the twins, Elijah and Elisha," Elizabeth continued as she sewed.

"Well, Reverend Sam needed someone to look after the younger children, so I suppose having a few more didn't really matter," Izzy said thoughtfully.

Sam and Josh had several siblings, and had only been ten years old when their mother had died in 1783; an eight year old sister, a five year old sister and a three year old brother had still been at home. Their older sisters had been young teens and while they could cope to some extent, the firm hand of a mother figure had been needed.

The Reverend Sturdevant had quickly remarried, to Sarah Beeman Morris, and she had capably served in the capacity of mother for several years. However, Sarah had died a short while before Izzy's initial visit to the past, and the Reverend had once more been at quite a loss.

Izzy remembered that at the time of her first 'visit,' the Reverend's young children had been given to a neighbor to look after, and the Reverend had spent much of his time with Sam and Elizabeth at their house. Maybe that neighbor had been the woman whom he had married just a year later.

"And he was lonely," Izzy added now in a gentle voice. She'd seen that for herself, the first time she had arrived at the Sturdevant home. "I'm glad he found Mrs. Cooley—what's her given name?" she asked.

"Ann-Lucy," Elizabeth answered shortly.

"You don't like her?" Izzy questioned, curious. Elizabeth's tone had been unusually clipped.

Elizabeth looked uncomfortable. "'Tis not so much that," she admitted slowly, clearly struggling with inner thoughts that she felt were counter-productive to her attempts to be a good Christian. "But she is so much younger than father-in-law," she said, adding that Ann-Lucy had been born in 1755. Izzy knew that the Reverend Sturdevant had been born in 1741.

"Hmmm—fourteen years is quite an age gap, even given the fact that these days men are often quite older than their wives, particularly second or third wives," Izzy agreed, missing Elizabeth's odd look at her rationalization, never mind the way she used 'gap,' which was only used of topographical formations at that time. "But he probably needed someone younger to run around after the children," Izzy concluded. "Is she nice?"

Elizabeth sighed. "She is," she declared, but the tone of her voice still suggested discomfort with her father in law's wife. "But—she just had yet another child," Elizabeth whispered, as though whispering the news would somehow make it less scandalous, as she apparently thought it was.

Izzy grinned. She wanted to say something congratulatory about the Reverend Sturdevant, at nearly sixty years old, still fathering children, but instinctively knew that Elizabeth wouldn't appreciate such a remark. Instead, she said, "well, that happens," and waited for Elizabeth to say more.

After a moment, Elizabeth said, "aye, but Ann-Lucy is nearly forty-five." She paused. "I could see the twin boys, after all, they had just been wed. But now, another child?"

Izzy laughed out loud. "You're thinking that they have enough!" She giggled. It was true: Josh and Sam had been one of nine children, Ann-Lucy had brought five of her own into the brood and then had proceeded to give birth to twins and now, another child.

Elizabeth smiled and nodded. "Only to you would I confess such uncharitable thoughts," she admitted. Then she sighed. "I have truly missed you, Izzy," she confessed, and gave Izzy a bright smile.

Izzy reached over and took Elizabeth's hand. "And I have missed you, Lizzie," she agreed. "Although I do have friends in Charlottesville...but none like you."

# CHAPTER EIGHT

"Tell me about Charlottesville," Elizabeth urged.

Izzy was only too happy to comply. She was deeply attached to Braintrim and to the house the Sturdevants lived in, and would always consider it her true home in this time, and this life. But she had discovered a more sophisticated and very vibrant society in the new city of Charlottesville, and was delighted to share some details with her friend.

"Charlottesville has been very logically planned," Izzy began complacently, confident in the perfection of her adopted home town. "The city is laid out in a square, more or less, and the roads and streets are parallel and perpendicular to each other, so it's very easy to find your way around. It is fifty acres," she continued.

"So large!" Elizabeth exclaimed, trying to envision such a big town.

Izzy nodded. "Indeed. The courthouse was set on the northern side of the town, and a big park—a public square with gardens and trees and so on—of two acres is in front of it. This part is on a little hill, so the courthouse looks down on the rest of the town." She giggled. "Joshua said that Dr. Walker, one of the Trustees responsible for the layout, made it that way so that people would always see Justice peering over their shoulders!"

Elizabeth laughed at her brother in law's wit.

"Around the square, as Josh told you last night, there are beginning to be all sorts of shops and offices. There are a couple of taverns as well, frequented by attorneys and others involved in courthouse business.

Our house is on the other side of the square, with another house to one side, and two more being built!" Izzy dearly wished that somehow she could show her sister in law a photograph of her new home, but she had to settle for a rough sketch, and a great deal of description.

Their home was a wood and brick townhouse, with a large kitchen, cold cellar and scullery below ground, reception rooms, a music room and a library on the ground floor, a ballroom, dining room, and two bed chambers on the next floor up, guest bed chambers on the next floor, and servants' rooms on the very top, in what Izzy thought of as the 'attic.' Fortunately, there was a small storage area up there as well as the rooms for the staff.

The nursery was on a half level, part way between the ballroom floor and the guest bed chamber floor, and could be accessed by a concealed doorway off the grand staircase and also by a door off the servants' stair. A third door led, through an intricate series of steps and landings, directly into Izzy and Josh's bed chamber, so that they could attend to their children easily and privately if need be. A small room housed within the nursery suite was Belinda's domain, as Nanny.

Taking some leaves from Jefferson's book, Izzy and Josh had designed their townhouse with both a front, or 'grand' stair to be used by the family and their friends and guests, and a back stair for the servants. While the latter was less ornate than the former, it was no less sturdy and just as safe and easy to mount.

There was also a 'dumb waiter' that brought food and other items between the kitchen and the dining room, and between the kitchen and the small pantry-like room on the main floor. This was handy if tea or other light refreshments were served in one of the reception rooms, so no one had to trudge up and down the stairways with laden trays.

The sanitary system in the Sturdevants' Charlottesville home was as modern as things got back in 1796, when the townhouse had been built. Although chamber pots were still used, the family had two privies for their comfort: a traditional outhouse at some distance from the rear door of the home, and a rather peculiarly styled one, right next to the rear door, connected by a short covered hallway. This was extremely convenient during the winter, and also generally eliminated any waiting for an available privy.

The peculiarity of this privy lay in the fact that Izzy had designed it with a small water tank near the ceiling and a pipe that led from it down to the toilet bowl area. Instead of a holding tank in the ground that was mucked out every month by the 'night soil man' this privy had a large ceramic bowl underneath the seat. An opening at the bottom of the bowl was connected by a fitted wooden pipe to the cesspit underneath the traditional outhouse. After using the privy, one merely pulled a chain at the side of the water tank to lift the stopper and start the flow of water down to the bowl and out through the pipe. It wasn't exactly a flush toilet, but it was as close as Izzy could get with the existing technology.

"Where on earth did you get that idea?" Elizabeth asked, wrinkling her nose as Izzy described the unusual outhouse.

Izzy just smiled and explained that because their townhouse had a drilled well that provided them with excellent water, it made filling the tank atop the back door privy relatively easy. If users were not profligate with their 'flushing' the tank could clean out the bowl several times before running dry.

Their staff did not have to go all the way to Vinegar Hill to the community well for water; had that been the case, Izzy's tank invention would not have been convenient.

"I asked Josh to design something similar for the kitchen," she told Elizabeth, whose eyes widened.

"You mean, to have clean running water at the pull of a lever, in the kitchen?"

Izzy nodded. "It's just cold water, and it comes gushing out of a pipe in the wall when one turns the handle, but it saves a great deal of time," she explained.

# CHAPTER NINE

While Izzy was regaling Elizabeth with the marvels of Charlottesville society as well as her own clever indoor plumbing devices, Josh and Sam were having a very serious discussion on politics.

Josh had quickly summarized for his twin at least part of his job as Chief Aide to John Marshall, one of the three men sent over in 1797 by President Adams to negotiate with France. He had not revealed every aspect, and all the duties, he'd been tasked with as Marshall's Aide, since much of it was confidential.

Josh had been, in effect, a spy. Only he, Izzy and Jefferson knew all the details of what he'd been asked to do and what he had done. Josh knew that, while he could tell Sam many things about his mission to France, he could not tell all, or reveal the real reason he had been placed in Marshall's entourage.

The French had been incensed over the US-England alliance forged by the Jay Treaty in 1794, and had begun raiding US merchant ships in retaliation. More than 300 ships had been seized, along with their goods, which not only got the French government's point across, the sale of the goods also helped raise money for their ongoing war —led by Napoleon— in Europe.

"That must have been intriguing," Sam agreed now of his twin's trip; he sounded a bit envious. "But we heard that the French Foreign Minister, Talleyrand, would not receive you!"

Josh nodded. "That is true. He sent emissaries in his stead, which would have been bad enough in and of itself," Josh explained. "But..."

His twin cut him off, clearly excited by the drama of the event. "We heard that the emissaries asked for money for Talleyrand, and a loan to the Directoire, before they would even start peace negotiations!" he put in, using the official name for the French government at the time.

Josh confirmed what his twin had heard, and enumerated staggeringly large sums.

The bribe to Talleyrand would have been about a quarter of a million dollars in contemporary money, and the loan to the French Government—at virtually no interest, too—would have equalled about ten million dollars. When Josh had shared the sums with Izzy, she had done the conversion, and the seriousness of the French emissaries' transgressions, and that of the Ambassador, had floored her.

"I am very glad we did not give in to their demands," Sam noted now with a nod of approbation. "I like John Marshall," he opined. "He seems like a very principled man, even if he is one of your Mr. Jefferson's chief opponents."

Sam's opinion was shared by many people in the United States, who had been pleased by Marshall's refusal to bow to the demands made by the French. Most U.S. citizens thought the French Minister's demands, once they learned of them, were outrageous and corrupt, and thought that his use of emissaries smacked of cowardice.

Few details of the mission or the French Ambassador's demands for a bribe and a loan to the government would have been made public at all, had it not been for Jefferson working behind the scenes. Jefferson had suspected that the mission to France would be highly controversial, which is why he'd wanted to have Josh, his 'eyes and ears,' embedded in Marshall's coterie.

Although Marshall initially had objected to a Jefferson protégé in his midst, Josh's qualifications and deferential demeanor, not to mention his fluency in French thanks to Izzy, had soon won him over.

Initially, President Adams had been prepared to tell the American people what was happening in France by releasing the Marshall envoys' letters back to the Capitol. However, because Josh had been specifically tasked by Jefferson to observe everything and report back to him, coded and secret messages were sent by Josh to the Vice President, detailing everything that occurred between the Marshall party and the French emissaries—and eventually the

Ambassador. So Jefferson had known even before Adams had known what was going on.

Cleverly, and to further his end of discrediting the President to enhance his own chances in the 1800 Presidential election, Jefferson had successfully convinced President Adams to keep the communiqués from France a secret. He had also told Adams that with the French already incensed over the Jay Treaty, publicly shaming the three French diplomats sent by the Ambassador to parlay with Marshall would only anger them further.

Because Adams did not want war with the French, or to instigate any further ill will or belligerent action, he agreed, and kept the Marshall communiqués confidential. But Jefferson suspected that this action would sow distrust among the citizens of the new country, and he had been correct.

Before long, Adams had been forced to make all the letters regarding the negotiations in France public. The President's completely independent brainwave about redacting the names of the French envoys had just played into Jefferson's larger aim to discredit him. The redaction had made Adams look a fool and worse, the American people had begun to distrust him.

Jefferson had hoped that trying to keep the missives secret would provoke a strong negative response from the citizenry of the new United States, and it had. But the redaction and the fallout from that had gone farther than even Jefferson might have imagined to discredit the President. Although the election was not until the following year, Adams lost favor over the incident, which had blown up in his face, and came derisively to be called 'The XYZ Affair.'

"He is a very intelligent man, even if he takes every opportunity to speak against Mr. Jefferson," Josh put in wryly now of Marshall. A leader in the Federalist Party, Marshall had been plucked from his seat in Congress to head up the negotiations in France.

"Then that must have been very difficult for you, being his Aide," Sam rejoined, "seeing how close you are with Mr. Jefferson."

Josh almost said something, but at the last minute bit his lip and merely nodded. "Aye."

"But this possible war between us and France. Are they serious?" Sam asked now, frowning.

Josh replied that the French had actually threatened to invade the United States if Marshall and his companions had not agreed to the bribe and the loan. "But we called Talleyrand's bluff when we sailed for home." Josh declared in satisfaction. "Asking for a bribe and a loan before negotiating is blackmail."

Sam nodded. " I am glad to hear you say that," he said. "The Jay Treaty gave England 'most favored nation' status, and I do understand why France was upset, even if I have not much use for the French, except for your Izzy."

Josh grinned. "The French wanted that status, too," he agreed.

"Of course. And you must also remember the long-standing enmity between France and England," Sam cautioned. He loved history, and although he had few books because books were scarce and precious, the ones he did have were all histories of Europe and the Orient, and maps of the world.

Josh nodded. "There is that. But I never understood why France did not merely seek to negotiate their own Jay Treaty, as it were, with us," he mused. "Until I met some of them: the French, I mean, and large groups of them, not just one or two, or the handful of refugees at Azilum," he continued. "Or Izzy," he added with a tender smile. "They are a stiff-backed lot!" he pronounced. "They refused to receive Ambassador Pinckney," he said, sounding outraged. "They would not ask for their own treaty, even though that would have been the logical thing to do, because to them, it would have seemed like being an also-ran, or a second best, to England. And they will not have that," he explained.

"But France's response, to seize our merchant ships in the West Indies, that was not the way to handle it," Sam put in, lighting his long pipe and taking a welcome puff. Fragrant smoke wafted into the air in the small front parlor where the men had gone for their discussion, knowing they would not be disturbed. A small fire crackled in the stone fireplace, and the space was scented with the holiday greenery that decorated the mantel and the windows.

"No. But seizing ships loaded with spices and other costly goods they can sell on the open market, or on the black market, is one way to raise cash," Josh reminded Sam.

They were silent for a long minute, both thinking.

Then Josh said, "Izzy has suggested that France may even go so far as to sell their holdings here, on this continent, to raise cash," he told his brother.

Sam looked askance. "I very much doubt that," he countered gravely. "Their holdings are vast, and they have thriving French populations in both Philadelphia and what was the Virginia County of Illinois. I do not suppose they would want to lose their foothold here, but rather gain *more* land."

Josh nodded. "Aye. Our Northwest Territory, of which Illinois is now a part, is vulnerable to French invasion since their holdings to the south provide a perfect gateway," Josh admitted. "So—might it not be best, if we could gain that land, to buy it from France? Should they be in such financial distress as to wish to, or be convinced to, sell it?" he asked.

Sam had to admit that the idea was sound, but he still said he could not imagine France wanting to give up so large a part of its presence in the New World.

Josh merely shrugged. " 'Tis Izzy's concept, and you know the way she sometimes seems to foretell things," he said quietly.

Sam nodded. "Aye. Were she not your wife, and indeed such a good, true, Christian soul, I should almost think her a witch!" Sam joked.

Josh had wanted to divulge Izzy's secret to his twin many times, but of course, he had never spoken of his remarkable wife's real past to anyone. He had promised Izzy, and would keep that promise. But sometimes, it made conversation difficult.

Now, he gave his twin a grin. "I do believe my wife is very intelligent and wise," he said honestly.

Sam nodded his agreement. Then: "President Adams does not want war with France, even though Mr. Hamilton and his party have done their best to stir up the people's feeling against the French," he offered, returning to the topic at hand. "But this business had not done him a credit."

Josh nodded. "Mr. Jefferson was most disappointed when he lost to President Adams," he confided to his twin.

In the 1796 election, in which Josh and Izzy had both worked on Thomas Jefferson's presidential campaign, Adams had garnered the most votes, with Jefferson coming in second. In the United States at that time, this meant Jefferson had become Vice President.

When Izzy and Josh married and moved to Charlottesville in 1796, part of the reason for their choice of home town was to be near Jefferson, with whom Josh worked closely. Jefferson, of course, was eyeing the Presidency, still, and intended to make a run at it in the coming year.

Izzy, who had known that Jefferson would lose to Adams in 1796 had of course not said a word to anyone about it. She hadn't even told Josh. She also knew, of course, that Jefferson would oust Adams in 1800, and so it was with a great deal of enthusiasm that she now was supporting their friend.

"Will Jefferson indeed stand, next year?" Sam queried, squinting through his pipe smoke to fix Josh with a bold stare. "He has a great deal of backing, and this whole affair with France has done much to damage President Adams," he reiterated.

Josh grinned at his brother's perspicacity: Sam was quite shrewd, especially in business and politics.

"Aye, I do believe he will."

Sam nodded. "'Twould be a fine thing, to have such a good friend of yours President!" he declared in a happy tone.

Josh had to agree.

"But why did the President try to keep the mission to France a secret, Josh? Do you know? Seems a very queer way to handle it: the President, and the government, works for the people. We have a right to know what they are doing, since they act on our behalf," Sam said staunchly.

Again, Josh nodded. "I agree completely, Sam," he said.  Josh could hardly tell his brother that the President's actions had been influenced by Jefferson's machinations behind the scenes, which in turn had been informed by his own undercover work in the Marshall coterie. "I do not have the President's confidence," he noted wryly, giving his brother a non-answer.

## CHAPTER TEN

Christmas Eve service at the Braintrim Church was held in the late afternoon. Tradition held that attendees would then return home and have a small festive supper: the major feasting, if one could afford it, would be done on Christmas Day itself, following Church services in the morning.

Thus it was that as the weak late December sun sank in the West, the four Sturdevants decided to walk the half mile to the church, since most of the snow that had fallen the day and evening before had melted. It was a fine, crisp afternoon, with no wind.

As they walked, the conversation still centered on Josh and Izzy's life in Charlottesville. Although Sam and Josh had finished talking politics, *per se,* they now discussed the Marshalls, whom Josh and Izzy had come to know well.

"Mrs. Marshall is a lovely lady, is she not, Izzy?" Josh prompted his wife as they made their way along the roadway's edge. A carriage or two passed them as they headed West into the village, and a couple of other people straggled out of the homesteads and farm houses to make their way into town, but mostly the Sturdevants had the road to themselves.

Izzy smiled and agreed. "While Josh and Mr. Marshall were both in France, Mrs. Marshall and I naturally gravitated towards each other," she admitted. "Polly—Mrs. Marshall— became quite a friend. Although she is a few years older than I am, she is interested in her husband's career, just as I'm interested in Josh's," Izzy explained. "Plus, I admire the way she and Mr. Marshall are devoted to each other. D'you know, she wears a locket 'round her neck with a lock of his hair in it? Isn't that romantic?" she asked.

"There is quite an age difference between them," Josh put in, completely innocent of the discussion his wife had had with Elizabeth earlier that day.

"Yes, but they do get on very well," Izzy countered, sliding a look at Elizabeth's face as they walked.

Elizabeth met her gaze, and gave a little smile.

Then Izzy chuckled. "I'd say they get on extremely well, as they keep having babies!" she declared. "As a matter of fact, Polly —Mrs. Marshall— is with child now, and little John is not yet two..."

"How many children have they?" Elizabeth asked, interested in spite of the nearness of the topic to her own father in law's situation, which made her uncomfortable. "And how much older than Mrs. Marshall is Mr. Marshall, do you know?" she queried.

Izzy thought for a moment. "Four living, with a fifth on the way. And Mr. Marshall is eleven years older than Polly—Mrs. Marshall."

" 'Tis wonderful to have a large family," Elizabeth said, then, hopping lightly over a slushy puddle. Her voice was tinged with longing.

Izzy moved from Josh's side to her sister in law's and put an arm around Elizabeth's shoulders. "You will have more children, Lizzie, I'm sure of it!" she whispered confidently.

Elizabeth smiled, and looked happy. "And I suppose a difference of age may not be so very great, if the two people involved truly respect and esteem each other," she conceded, though she still had her own private doubts.

The Christmas Eve service was one of great joy and anticipation, the church itself festooned with greenery and smelling of pine, and beeswax from the many candles.  They sang several songs, most of which Izzy knew although the tunes to some of them, particularly 'Come Thou Long Expected Jesus,' were different. 'Christians Awake' and 'While Shepherds Watched Their Flocks' were familiar though.

On the walk home, the stars above the four Sturdevants were very bright in the dark sky, and the Milky Way was clearly visible.

"What a beautiful night!" Izzy remarked, squeezing Josh's arm a little more tightly. "I think it very grand indeed that your church has a pipe organ!" Izzy continued happily. "It adds so much to the singing."

Elizabeth, walking just ahead with her arm through Sam's, agreed, and said that the organ had been sent as a memorial bequest from a wealthy family whose matriarch had been a faithful member of the Reverend Sturdevant's flock.

It was so quiet and still, the only sound was the noise their shoes made on the chilled, packed earth road, and Elizabeth's quiet voice carried easily.

"I was disappointed not to hear 'Joy to the World,' though," Izzy confessed. "Or do we sing that tomorrow?" she asked, knowing there was a Christmas Day service as well.

Elizabeth looked over her shoulder and frowned, her face puzzled. " 'Joy to the World?'" she echoed, and hummed a couple of bars. "That tune?"

Izzy nodded. She knew it had been written by Isaac Watts who had used Handel's *Messiah* as inspiration. Both Watts and Handel had lived in the late seventeenth and early eighteenth century, and their music was well known by now.

Knowing the Braintrim church's strong tradition of music, and having attended only makeshift services in Charlottesville which had neither an organ or a real church, Izzy had been looking forward to what she considered a 'real' Christmas service, hymns and all.

"But—Izzy, surely, that is a tune rejoicing in the Second Coming," Elizabeth gently corrected her. "'Tis not a hymn celebrating Our Lord's birth."

Izzy bit her lip and mumbled something about just liking it anyway, and everyone walked on towards the Sturdevant home.

Oops, Izzy thought to herself. She hadn't known that about 'Joy to the World.' Oh well, she didn't think any damage had been done.

When they returned, it took Martha and Becky just a few minutes to set out the special supper she had prepared ahead, and which Elizabeth had designed particularly for Izzy. After gathering in the small upstairs parlor for little glasses of sherry, which went a long way to ward off any chill they might have taken during the walk home, the Sturdevants moved into the dining room, where candles had been lit and all the food had been placed.

A snowy white table cloth covered the table, and Elizabeth had put out her best china, silver and glassware, which sparkled and gleamed.

"Oh, how lovely!" Izzy exclaimed. For the church service and this festive dinner afterwards, she had donned one of the silk gowns she'd bought in London on her honeymoon. Despite having birthed two children, the gown still fit well, in part because of the Empire waist design. The fabric was a 'watered' silk in a deep pewter, and tiny crystals were scattered here and there across the entire garment.

Elizabeth, in a gown of navy silk trimmed with embroidered vines, beamed. "I am so happy to have a chance to use these things," she said quietly. "Tomorrow we shall use them again, although the children will have more—serviceable—table ware," she added in a murmur and Izzy realized that with the Reverend Sturdevant's large and mostly young family, the best china and glassware might not be the best choice for all the diners. She was also honored that Elizabeth had put out her best for their Christmas Eve supper.

"Ah, now, what have we here?" asked Sam as they all sat in their places. To give the servants the evening at liberty, the supper had been set out, but it would be up to Elizabeth, as hostess, to serve.

Beaming, Elizabeth began to point to the covered dishes and explain what they would be eating. "'Tis not after a Midnight service, but 'tis as close as we might come here to the French tradition of the Réveillon," she began with a look to Izzy.

"A Réveillon!" Izzy repeated, overcome.

All at once she realized that, since Lizzy of course thought she was a French noblewoman and a Catholic, the tradition of the Réveillon would have been something from her past which she might be presumed to treasure. Izzy also realized the trouble Elizabeth had gone to in arranging and obtaining the particular dishes associated with this celebration. And she recalled from her own modern childhood the time honored Réveillon dinner as produced by her own grandmother.

"Sure I am 'tis not as grand as what you had in France," Elizabeth began gently, but Izzy interrupted her.

"Oh, Lizzy it's perfect!" she gasped, dashing a tear from her eye and hugging her sister in law. "How on earth…?"

Glowing with delight, Elizabeth explained that she and Sam had contacted the Charriers from Azilum, who had given her the list of dishes most usual at the Réveillon feast, and then recipes for the ones she and Martha had chosen.

"We had the salmon and lobster brought wrapped in seaweed and on ice from New York," Sam noted expansively. "It being winter time, it was not too difficult." He grinned. "Obtaining enough cocoa to make the dessert was fortunately an easy thing as well, although using it as a confection rather than a drink is something of a departure, I am given to understand from Martha," he added.

"She went to some pains to obtain the cocoa butter, from a specialty purveyor," Elizabeth put in. "We made three batches of the chocolate sauce before it was the way we thought it should be," she told Izzy with a grin, who was still staring in admiration and quite in the grip of her emotions. "It was delicious work!"

There was chilled smoked salmon, a lobster casserole with the ever popular macaroni, and the famous tourtière meat pie. For dessert, Martha had made her version of a 'Bûche de Noël' which turned out to be layers of chocolate cake interspersed with cream frosting and covered with a chocolate ganache. To drink, Lizzy and Sam had broken out the last bottle of the St. Hilaire Champagne that Thomas Jefferson had brought years before for Izzy and Josh's wedding, and served it, crisp and cold, in the cut crystal glasses.

"I wanted to make it very special and to make you feel at home," Elizabeth told Izzy quietly.

Josh, who had been apprised of the scheme beforehand, just smiled.

"Oh, I do feel at home," Izzy said, her voice cracking with happiness. "But it is all of you who are special."

## CHAPTER ELEVEN

Christmas Day, the Sturdevants took their carriage into town to attend the morning church service. Then, whisked home in good time, they readied the house to welcome Elizabeth's parents Ebenezer and Eunice Skinner, as well as the Reverend Sturdevant, his wife, and their several children who were all coming to Christmas Dinner and to spend the afternoon.

Izzy wore a bright emerald green brocaded silk dress with the fashionably high waistline, puffed sleeves and low neck. Because the temperature in the house could vary, she tucked a snowy white lace fichu in the neck of her gown and tossed a silk shawl in deep rose over her shoulders. White gloves—which she would probably carry more than wear, since they were *en famille*, after all, completed her ensemble.

Elizabeth's pale blonde hair was set off by her light blue watered silk dress. It had ribbons of a silvery material at its high waist, and the puffed sleeves were decorated in vertical stripes with more of the silver fabric. She had a gossamer silk fichu in a matching pale blue at her throat, and a knitted shawl of fine royal blue wool around her shoulders.

Both women wore lacy caps: Elizabeth's had two rows of ruffles around its edge while Izzy's, which was crooked more often than not, was of snow white *point de Gaze*.

Josh and Sam both wore white linen shirts, white silk cravats, embroidered waistcoats and frock coats. Josh's waistcoat was navy and gold, and his coat was a deep golden wool. He wore long navy trousers, whereas Sam wore cream colored breeches and hose with a maroon and gold waistcoat and a dark brown coat. Josh noticed his twin eyeing his long trousers, much as he had upon their arrival, and knew that eventually Sam would comment once more on this 'newfangled' fashion.

Martha, Ephraim, Becky, Belinda and Roger had readied the house quickly that morning after attending the earliest service, and remained at home with the children while the adults went to church.

Elizabeth's parents had no children still at home, so visited each of their offspring's homes in turn during the holidays, beginning with Elizabeth's, which was nearest their own home.

Jesse, the youngest full sibling of Sam and Josh by their father and his first wife, was nineteen and still at home and unwed. He was working on his father's large farm, and would be coming to dinner.

Ann-Lucy , the Reverend's new wife, had three of her five children from her first marriage still at home, so they would also be coming. The twin boys who were now two and the infant daughter who was just six months old would also be present.

Sam and Josh's other siblings all lived at some distance and would likely visit their father's home during the Christmas 'twelve day' holiday period that ended after New Year's.

It was a joyous reunion, for Izzy hadn't seen Reverend Sturdevant for three years, and nor, of course, had Josh.

"Ah, my son, you be doing fine work for our nation, fine work," noted the Reverend, pumping his son's hand and smiling as Martha eased off his cloak and took his broad brimmed hat.

Josh grinned: he'd kept in touch with his father through letters which, although they had been purposely vague about details, had nonetheless given the elder Sturdevant a good idea about what his son had been up to in Washington and Virginia, and most lately, in France.

The Reverend Sturdevant spied Izzy, standing a little bit behind her husband, and regarding the reunion with brimming eyes. Even though she was just a daughter in law, and a rather unusual sort of person whom he'd thought quite odd at first, Izzy now held a special place in the Reverend's heart. He enveloped her in a huge hug, completely out of character for him.

"You be looking very well, my girl, very well," he told her in a tone of great satisfaction, and exclaimed over their children—his grandchildren, whom he was meeting for the first time— just as Sam and Elizabeth had.

"It's so wonderful to see you, Reverend Sam," Izzy said genuinely, taking the older man's hand. She was the only one he allowed to use this diminutive: everyone else called him 'Sir' or ' Reverend Sturdevant' or 'Father.' "But you look a bit—tired. Are you quite well?" she asked quietly.

The arrival of Mrs. Reverend Sturdevant and all the children had created a bit of a hubbub in the Keeping Room, and Izzy drew her father in law off to one side and earnestly examined his face in the clear light by a window.

"Christmas is a tiring time for all clergy," the Reverend replied with a smile. "And there has been some—trouble— in the church," he continued hesitantly. "Did not Sam and Elizabeth tell you?" he queried.

Izzy shook her head and bit her lip: she and Josh had been so busy sharing the wonders of their trip to England and life in Charlottesville they had hardly had time to hear about Sam and Elizabeth's world here in Braintrim.

"Well, no matter." The Reverend sighed wearily. "'Tis not a subject for so joyous a day."

"Oh, but Josh and I want to know—maybe we can help!" Izzy declared with the confidence and optimism of the content.

Reverend Sturdevant smiled at her. He would never forget this unusual girl's sudden and odd appearance at this very house that warm summer day four years before, never forget her kindness to him, either, as he had struggled with mourning the death of his wife and the need to find a new mother for his children. Those two things had been so distinctly at odds, he had felt torn, conflicted and unable to make progress in either matter.

Izzy had seemed to understand the world instinctively, and had also offered at times rather uncanny insights.

She was peculiar, of that the Reverend Sturdevant was sure, and further acquaintance with her during the months she had spent with Sam and Elizabeth prior to Izzy's marriage with Josh had only convinced the Reverend Sturdevant more completely of that. But he had no doubt about how much his son Josh loved Izzy. And time had also increased his respect for her, whom he now regarded as one of the most intelligent, kind and thoughtful ladies he had ever had the good fortune to encounter.

Ebenezer and Eunice Skinner arrived on the heels of the Reverend Sturdevants and soon the adults were gathered in the River Room while the children stayed in the Keeping Room under the watchful eyes of Martha, Becky, Ephraim, Roger, Belinda and Jesse, who quite enjoyed keeping his younger siblings entertained and well behaved. He was also having fun getting to know his nephew Nicholas and little Cordelia.

While the infants played with balls of yarn and wooden animals and the older children worked on puzzles, Jesse, Ephraim and Roger entered into a spirited discussion on the ethics of slavery. They found themselves of similar mind on the matter, which seemed to forge a fast and quick, though unlikely, camaraderie among them.

The only adult guest Izzy had not met before, besides Jesse, was Ann-Lucy Brown Cooley Sturdevant, the Reverend's new wife. Married later in the same summer as Josh and Izzy had been, Mrs. Reverend Sturdevant had been a widow whom Izzy assessed had been only too glad to accept the Reverend Sturdevant's proposal. A widow's lot, even with a dead husband's pension, was a grim one, especially with several children to provide for.

Although Elizabeth had expressed doubt about her new mother in law, Izzy saw only that 'Lucy'—as her husband called her— Sturdevant was a capable and devoted mother, treating all her children in a loving and fair manner. Was she a bit distracted and frazzled, as Izzy would say? Yes, to be sure. But with that many young children, plus an infant and twin toddlers, who wouldn't be? Izzy did not doubt, as she thought Elizabeth might, that Ann-Lucy cared greatly for her husband.

The Reverend Sturdevant sat with his wife on a love seat in one corner of the River Room, and Sam, Josh and Izzy took turns sitting on a small chair near by and conversing with them.

Izzy knew that Elizabeth's discomfort over her father in law's new wife came mostly from the fact that Ann-Lucy was fourteen years younger than the Reverend, and from the fact that she was increasing the Reverend's family on an almost yearly basis with children who were the same age as Elizabeth's own. Elizabeth had also confided in her that she had wondered if Ann-Lucy had not seized upon the Reverend's proposal as a convenient solution to her financial strictures, for although the Reverend was not rich, he owned a great deal of land and was connected to people like his son Sam, who were quite well off. Elizabeth had not seemed certain that the Reverend's new wife truly cared for him.

These situations, unusual perhaps but in no way improper, would just take getting used to, Izzy thought. She hoped that Elizabeth might, in time, come to feel fondly towards Ann-Lucy. And watching Ann-Lucy with the Reverend now, Izzy thought that at the very least the woman esteemed and respected the Reverend, which, if not love, was a good beginning.

Although Elizabeth was happy to see her mother Eunice, it was clear she was closer to her father, Ebenezer, who still doted on his daughter. The two of them took every opportunity to converse between themselves, clearly sharing a delight in subjects they both enjoyed, and in speaking with each other.

Eunice seated herself on one end of a long padded settee that afforded a fine view of the wintry Susquehanna that sparkled grey and white in the December sun. Izzy, noting that Sam and Josh were both chatting with their father and Ann-Lucy, and that Elizabeth and her father were exclaiming over a bound book of mounted butterflies and moths and recalling times long past when together they had chased and captured the creatures, went over and sat next to Eunice.

After a couple of awkward fumbles during which Izzy tried to figure out the older woman's interests, the two women began an intense discussion of European fashion, Napoleon's wife Josephine, and how the new Classical-inspired designs in clothing related to the equally new philosophy of Rational Enlightenment.

Izzy was quite surprised to find someone so conversant with au courant fashion and philosophy here in rural Pennsylvania, then chided herself for assuming that someone, if they were motivated enough, couldn't find the means to inform themselves about such things.

There were depths to Eunice Culver Skinner that Izzy had never expected, having only met her briefly during the summer she had arrived, and around the time of Elizabeth's first lying in. She found she quite enjoyed the conversation, and was almost sorry when Martha discreetly motioned to Elizabeth that the Christmas Feast was ready.

# CHAPTER TWELVE

Dinner was amazing. Izzy and Josh had attended some mighty fancy feasts and parties in Charlottesville and at Monticello and neighboring mansions. But in Izzy's opinion, the Christmas Day dinner put on by Martha, Ephraim and Becky with last minute help from Belinda and Roger, could take pride of place alongside the finest.

Izzy had learned to be satisfied with a somewhat different sort of Christmas celebration here in the past. In this era, the emphasis was on special food and drink and socializing with family and friends. Decorations were minimal: some greenery throughout the house generally sufficed. And that had been the hardest for Izzy to get used to: she missed a big Christmas Tree with all sorts of lights and ornaments. She missed candy canes. And, frankly, she missed the secularized Santa Claus.

But she had told her own children about the historical Saint Nicholas, and the later tradition of leaving their shoes out on December fifth for him to fill with candy, so that helped assuage her longing to a degree.

The Sam Sturdevants' Christmas Dinner was done in fine tradition: the long cherry wood dining table had been polished to a luster and the center was graced by a grouping of fat beeswax candles nestled in an arrangement of white pine branches, pine cones and some sprigs of variegated, berried holly. Similar greens decorated the fireplace's mantel, as did more candles, and the windows' sills held small bunches of the greenery too. Another ball of mistletoe, this one in a white ribbon, hung in the doorway that led to the upstairs of the house.

Elizabeth had once again put out her best silverware: a set of Georgian sterling that had been her mother's mother's family: the style was plain and not monogrammed, but the quality shone elegantly. The china was also Elizabeth's best, a Spode 'Stoke China' which would later be re-named 'bone china' in a Japanese-inspired pattern of red, cream and blue tones with gilt accents. The service for eight had been another wedding gift from her parents.

It might have been a bit much for rural Pennsylvania, Izzy thought to herself as she entered the dining room, but nothing was too good for Ebenezer Skinner's darling daughter. She smiled as she saw Ebenezer and Elizabeth exchange a gleeful smile.

Izzy fingered the beautiful tableware almost reverently: she and Josh had chosen their own 'best' china and flatware, too, which she loved: an Oriental patterned Coalport bone china service and flatware from Paul Revere. (Yes, *the* Paul Revere, a fact that still gave Izzy goosebumps.) But Elizabeth's table was undeniably beautiful. Crystal water goblets and delicate wine glasses completed each place setting.

The shutters had been thrown wide and the weak but determined late December sun slanted into the dining room, gilding whatever it touched as it headed towards the western horizon. The scent of pine and burning firewood mingled with the smells emanating from the kitchen and ovens below in the Keeping Room, and Izzy's mouth watered as she and Josh took their places at the long table.

Because there were so many children, as well as an ample number of servants, and because Jesse had volunteered to stay with the younger guests, the children had their own special table, dressed in a bright red cloth with pure white plates and mugs, in the Keeping Room, where they would have Christmas Dinner. Becky, Belinda, Roger, Ephraim and Martha also had their Christmas Dinner there with the children and Jesse and from the laughter and cheerful chatter that wafted up the stairs to the Dining Room, it was by all accounts an excellent occasion.

Upstairs in the Dining Room, Sam sat at one end of the long table, and Elizabeth at the other. He beamed at her over the candles and greens as everyone sat down.

To Elizabeth's right was Reverend Sturdevant, and to Sam's right was Elizabeth's mother.  To

Reverend Sturdevant's right—to his delight—was Izzy, and to her right was Elizabeth's father, Ebenezer. To Eunice's right and across from Izzy was Josh, and to his right was Ann-Lucy.

Although Izzy had become used to the rather rigid protocol of speaking first to the person on your right and then to the person on your left during formal and political dinners in Virginia, here there was no such rule, and everyone spoke to the others as they desired. Still, it was Elizabeth's lookout as hostess to be certain no one was ignored or felt slighted, and to guide the conversation out of tricky waters should it enter into subjects that could be upsetting. After dinner there would be plenty of opportunity for everyone to talk more deeply and more frankly, but dinner was the time to encourage conviviality and promote good digestion.

They began with a creamy oyster chowder in shallow, wide-rimmed bowls. It was indulgently rich and brightened with spices and herbs, including nutmeg and thyme. Next came small plates of broiled river herring accompanied by tiny whole pickled beetroot, boiled pearl onions and spiced cucumbers the size of Izzy's little finger. With these dishes was served a fairly dry white wine imported from France that Sam had gone to some trouble to obtain.

Next came a large roast turkey with chestnut stuffing, a platter of Roast beef with Yorkshire

Pudding, and a huge Virginia Ham that Izzy and Josh had sent on ahead to be part of the feast. Alongside the meats were lima beans, baked acorn squash with brown sugar, sweet potatoes baked with cranberries and spices, and various tangy sauces such as horseradish and green pepper.

Izzy took a spoonful of everything, because it was just too good to pass up. She held her glass out for some of the bright claret that Sam was proudly pouring to go with this portion of the dinner, and thought to herself that the current Empire waisted fashion in ladies' dresses was certainly convenient at big dinners!

Although it seemed impossible, once everyone had had their fill of the meats and vegetables—and by now, the sun was starting to edge behind the trees on the far western horizon—the dessert selection was presented. Martha and Becky had baked the usual mincemeat, walnut, and apple pies so that everyone could have their favorite. But there were also peaches in brandy, a steamed plum pudding, 'Indian' pudding, and two types of cupcakes: precious, sweet chocolate and rich vanilla. Both were topped with a thick, ivory buttercream-type of icing and decorated with candied ginger and orange peel.

Cupcakes were a relatively new concept, having first been mentioned in Amelia Simmons' 1796 'American Cookery,' of which Izzy had a copy. She had managed to send a second copy to Elizabeth and Martha's Christmas Cupcakes were the result.

With dessert, Sam served madeira and port, and there were small dishes of nuts on the table as well, as though the diners would need anything else to eat!

Once everyone appeared to have had, at last, their fill, Elizabeth stood and led the rest of the ladies into the front parlor, leaving the gentlemen to more port and a discussion, no doubt, of politics and other weighty matters.

# CHAPTER THIRTEEN

The ladies' conversation, although ensconced in the soft pastel tones of the front parlor, was no less grave, since Izzy began by asking Ann-Lucy about the problems in the church that Reverend Sturdevant had mentioned. That lady, who wore a deep aubergine dress in the current fashion and an ivory lace cap with somewhat unbecoming—if fashionable—'lappets', seemed only too eager to share the difficulty that had been plaguing the Reverend of late. Her round face adopted a worried look as she began to speak, and her grey eyes were grave.

"My good husband has wrestled many an hour with the problem," she began, shooting a tremulous smile at Izzy, and including Eunice and Elizabeth in her glance. She explained that many years before, when the United States was still a collection of British Colonies, the king, George III, had granted land in what would become Pennsylvania to various families in Connecticut. At that time, she said, sections of Pennsylvania were considered to be part of Connecticut.

Not long after, William Penn, for whom Pennsylvania was named, also deeded huge tracts of land to various settlers. Unfortunately, it was the same land, although the tracts were so great and the population so sparse, the issue had not immediately been noticed.

In some cases, the dispute had been settled amicably, but in others it had grown to be contentious. Such it was now between two members of the Reverend Sturdevant's Braintrim Baptist Church, who had lately discovered that they both owned the same 700 acre parcel of land: one through a family deed from George III and the other through a family deed from William Penn.

"'Tis the future of the parcel of land which has caused so much dissension," Ann-Lucy told her audience in a worried tone. She sipped at the cup of savory darjeeling that Elizabeth had served her. The land in question, it turned out, was on the opposite shore of the Susquehanna from Laceyville in an area that Izzy knew would come to be called Quick's Bend. But the Quick family had only a couple of representatives in that area at this time.

Each party who claimed to own the land felt that the spot would be ideal for a river ferry crossing, of which there were very few. Additionally, the curvature of the river at that point meant that the overland distance between settlements was considerably shorter, and a direct road linking the settlements was planned.

For these reasons, it was presumed that Quick's Bend was likely to become a lucrative holding, with both road tolls and ferry fees a source of income, and with businesses seeking to locate there because of the ease of transportation. Hence the acerbity of the dispute.

"I suspect that it is because the disagreement is motivated by revenue that Reverend Sturdevant is so troubled," Izzy commented, choosing her words carefully. She didn't want to say 'greed' but from Ann-Lucy's recounting that was precisely the motivating factor.

Everyone nodded assent.

"He has prayed and prayed and asked the Lord for guidance," Ann-Lucy whispered, and shook her head. "But still they persist in their enmity, going on two years now."

"Mr. Skinner has said that the Reverend Sturdevant will call a church council after Christmas," Eunice put in, her voice sympathetic. Her pale gold hair, not unlike her daughter's, was wound around her head in elaborate braids that disappeared beneath her embroidered cap, and the bodice of her navy brocade gown rose and fell with the emotion of her breathing. "Perhaps that will assist in the peace making."

All but Izzy looked hopeful: she knew from her modern day research that the dispute would go on for more than a decade, and would mean that a handful of members would leave and go to another church because of the rupture. The following year, 1800, the wider Baptist Church Association would even think that the Braintrim church had disbanded over the dispute. But through it all, she knew the Reverend Sturdevant would continue to preach and hold fast to his faith, and be rewarded when the wayward members but one returned and were accepted back into the fold at Braintrim.

Time, Izzy reflected, could distance and diminish disagreements. In this case, modern source material had given her very few details of the disruption they were now discussing: indeed, she was surprised to learn the names of the parties involved from Ann-Lucy, because no modern sources had revealed them.

She would have to wait and see what finally would make the two families come to a compromise over the property. Izzy suspected that one of the parties in the dispute might die during the coming years, and that his heirs would not be so adamant, and reach a civil compromise.

Or, perhaps, it would be determined that the Quick's Bend area might not be such a good place for an overland road and a ferry: in modern times, there was no such direct overland road, and Izzy knew that within two years, a Laceyville area ferry would be up and running, and within a half century ferries would operate near Wyalusing and Meshoppen.

Additionally, toll bridges would be erected at Laceyville and Wyalusing. So with the disputed land's prospects becoming less valuable, maybe the arguing parties would see compromise as a more reasonable outcome.

"And every day I pray to God for peace among our flock, as well, and to bring an untroubled mind to my good husband," Ann-Lucy finished quietly. "For he has been so vexed and I can do nothing." She paused and blinked several times very rapidly.

Everyone held their breath and was completely silent. Elizabeth looked taken aback.

"But surely, no one expects *you* to solve the problem," Elizabeth told her step-mother in law gently.

Izzy was glad to hear Elizabeth speak that way to Ann-Lucy.

Ann-Lucy gave a tremulous smile. "I comprehend, Elizabeth," she replied, soft. "But you see, my good husband's happiness is my every wish and desire. And when it is not within my power to serve him and make him happy, I feel at a loss."

Elizabeth nodded, but inside, her brain was working very fast. Had she perhaps misjudged Ann-Lucy? And was that the root of it, in truth: that she had judged her—a most un-Christian thing to do!

True, she did not know the woman extremely

well, and true, they had both been very busy with their own families and confinements in the few years Ann-Lucy had been part of the Sturdevant family. So there had been little opportunity to get to know each other.

But maybe the twin boys, and now the new daughter, were not just babies Ann-Lucy had wished to have to cement her new union with the Reverend —an un-charitable thought the Elizabeth hadn't been able to voice, even to Izzy, and was ashamed to admit now to herself. Maybe the Reverend Sturdevant had wanted more children. He had always said that next to God, his family was his greatest joy, and if it had been possible, the Reverend had seemed more jubilant at the arrival of little John, and then Peter, than Sam and Elizabeth herself.

With a clearer mind and renewed compassion for Ann-Lucy, Elizabeth smiled, and returned to the conversation.

# CHAPTER FOURTEEN

While the ladies discussed the schism in the church, and then turned to less troublesome subjects, such as children, books, music and new fashion, the men had remained in the dining room with their port and pipes. Sam and Ebenezer were the only ones who smoked, both drawing similar long pipes out, and filling them with fragrant tobacco. And the Reverend had chosen mulled cider *in lieu* of the alcoholic beverages offered.

Their talk began with a brief and joyless update on the same subject their ladies had discussed: the Braintrim church schism.

"I am truly at my wits' end," admitted Reverend Sturdevant in a somber voice. "And failing my own poor wits, of course, I have continually asked God for help in this affliction."

"And surely God will answer your prayer, Father," Sam put in encouragingly.

"'Tis over land," Ebenezer chimed in. "Land, and money, for land, as you well know, *is* money."

The Reverend Sturdevant nodded his big grey head. "And that is what troubles me more deeply than the fact that two of my own flock have come to such bitter enmity. That it is a matter of money. The love of money is, truly, the root of all evil." He sighed.

"Aye, Father. We will all pray for a resolution," Sam offered.

"I am calling a church council for January," the Reverend Sturdevant announced, nodding at the faces gathered around him.

"Well, let us hope and pray that it will be productive," Ebenezer commented.

Then the four men turned to a much lengthier report on current and proposed businesses in the area, mostly for Josh's benefit.

"It is hard to believe that there is a hotel now, in Braintrim!" Josh declared wonderingly. "And a cabinet maker as well as the furniture maker?"

"Aye—the cabinet maker's pieces are those requiring more skill and fancy work," Sam explained. "And as for the hotel, there is also a small rooming house, for long-term guests," he elaborated.

"The draper has expanded," commented Ebenezer. "Good thing, too: 'tis now much easier for me to get supplies, since there is more commerce in town."

Josh nodded, realizing that a full barge coming up stream was certainly more cheerfully and readily sent than one that carried only some of the cargo it was able to.

They discussed the two mills that Sam owned, and Sam returned again to the topic of fabric mills.

Although they had never seen such an establishment, Sam had read extensively on them, and enlightened his listeners, stressing the benefits of starting such an operation.

"Certainly, with a rooming house now, we could offer lodgings to the workers," he said enthusiastically. "And more people would mean a need for more shops, bigger shops, and perhaps an eatery of some kind."

"More than a tavern, you mean?" Ebenezer was quick to ask. He respected his son in law's business acumen and was always anxious to seize on any forecasts Sam might be willing to make.

Sam nodded and tamped down his pipe tobacco. "Aye." He added that he had read that in France, stand-alone restaurants, not attached to a bar or tavern, nor part of an inn, hotel or similar, had begun to crop up.

"Leave it to the French!" joked Josh, who was the only one of the party safe to make such a comment, since he was married to a Frenchwoman.

Everyone chuckled.

"There has also been talk in the village," Sam went on, "about establishing our own Assembly Hall here." He looked apologetically at Ebenezer. "Some think 'tis too far to travel for evening meetings, to your Hall," he added in a gentle tone. "And there may be a donation of land on which to build."

Behind Ebenezer's Tavern the large multi-purpose Hall was the site of town meetings; any legal proceedings that required more room than the Magistrate's Office also took place there, and community dances and other events were held in the spacious Hall. However, what Sam was revealing now was that the village of Braintrim was considering building its own Hall.

"One of the Laceys, I should wager," Ebenezer commented gruffly, but with good humor. The Lacey family lived on a large tract of land beginning at the western edge of the center of the village of Braintrim. They had started with a single large farmhouse where Isaac and his wife Lydia still lived, but now his father Ebenezer had come from Connecticut to Braintrim, too, and settled in a second home not far from Isaac and Lydia's.

Isaac and his wife had been blessed with several children, all of whom helped work the very large farm comprising several hundred acres; by now, a couple of the older children had married and settled in yet more homes built on the property, all an easy distance from the principle homestead.

Although most of the Laceys were weavers— the family owned the draper's shop in the village, too — woodworkers or farmers, they owned so much land, and now had so many grown children employed in other businesses and pursuits, that they were quickly becoming the most prominent family in the village.

"Aye," Sam acknowledged with a grin. He lowered his voice. "I call it the Lacey Compound," he said of the vast tracts of land and several dwellings of the family. "And they have enough land to give a bit to the village for an Assembly Hall, and perhaps a central office for the Magistrate as well, and the Sheriff," he added. The Sheriff had his office in the front part of his home just east of the village center, but the Magistrate lived at some distance, on a hillside out of town. A central location for all of the village's community activities might be quite convenient.

Ebenezer sighed. "It could be a good idea, Sam, because thanks in no small part to your mills and your business ideas, the Eddy itself is becoming, with Black Walnut Bottom, a thriving hamlet. Mayhap within a generation it would only be good sense for each community to have its own Hall and council."

"Avoiding the lower-lying lands, many have cleared and built homes and shops towards the hills, the higher ground," Reverend Sturdevant put in. His own home was between the area known as 'Skinner's Eddy' and Black Walnut Bottom, on a low rise that kept it safe from any floodwaters of the Susquehanna

River. "And we have begun our own cemetery, as you know," he added quietly. His late wife had been the first burial at the Black Walnut Cemetery, as it had been deemed to far to go to the Braintrim Village Cemetery, located on the southwestern border of the village, along the river, more than five miles away.

Although both Black Walnut and the Eddy had been settled by pioneers for more than a century, the floodwaters had proven problematical. Thus, some traveled west, towards Braintrim Village where Dr. William Hooker Smith had built one of the first houses—the very house they all were in! Others, like the DePews, had traveled north, up into the foothills of the low mountains of the Northern Tier of Pennsylvania, and established themselves there.

Josh listened avidly.

"'Twould indeed make sense. We have a larger population now, in both areas," Sam put in eagerly.

"Aye," Ebenezer confirmed.

"We would also need to have a tavern," Sam mused. "Or perhaps one of those more expanded 'restaurants,'" he added with a faraway look in his eye.

"I have heard talk among my fellow clergy from the Valley and elsewhere that regular weekly postal service is to be established here within a few years," the Reverend Sturdevant put in.

At the present time, mail came once every two weeks by Pony Express or river barge. Weekly service would be an amazing boon.

Sam was sketching the Braintrim Assembly Hall building in his mind: offices at one side for village officials, and a large open space that could hold all the meetings and events the town might ever need occupying the central area. At his father's words, he snapped out of his reverie.

"Mmm...we should need room for a post office, then," he murmured.

"Aye," his father in law agreed with a wave of his pipe stem.

"The Braintrim Village Post Office," Sam breathed. "Or perhaps, Braintrim Town?" he suggested.

Ebenezer gave a short chuckle. "More likely Lacey Town," he returned, "especially if they give the village the land."

The Reverend Sturdevant was nodding thoughtfully. "Hmmm....hmmmm...mmmm...Lacey Town, Lacey Village..." he looked up at his sons and his friend, Ebenezer. "No... 'Laceyville,'" he determined with a grin. "It has a fine ring to it."

## CHAPTER FIFTEEN

Some of the gifts brought by Izzy and Josh for their family were exchanged once the gentlemen rejoined the ladies after dinner. In the front parlor, the pale lemon walls were burnished by the firelight and the glow from several candelabra that had been brought in from the dining room. A large mirror over the mantel reflected the light as well and everyone seemed cheered and quite merry.

Ebenezer made 'flips,', blending rum, dried pumpkin that he had asked Martha for earlier, eggs and cream with just enough dark beer to make the mixture fizz. Then he poured the bisque colored liquid back and forth between two pitchers several times.

Elizabeth did not fear for her rug, for she knew her father was a consummate drinks master, and just a bit of a showman as the liquid flowed faultlessly between the two silver containers for the space of several breaths.

Then Ebenezer poured the entire quantity into one pitcher, grabbed a hot fire poker he called a 'flip dog' and plunged it into the brew.

Izzy, intensely curious, peered into the silver pitcher to see the liquid froth and bubble as the poker singed it.

"Have you not tasted a flip in Charlottesville?" Ebenezer asked of Izzy, who admitted that she had not.

"'Tis perhaps a drink more common to taverns," he admitted. "And I should wager you do not frequent those," he added with a good humored smile.

Izzy giggled, and said that no, in Charlottesville she had not even seen the inside of a tavern, much less had a drink of any kind there.

"Well, go you with your Joshua, then, upon your return, and ask for a flip," Ebenezer instructed her as he poured the foaming stuff into balloon-shaped glasses and handed them around. "I am certain you shall find no finer flip anywhere than the one made by my own hand," he concluded with another smile, and handed her a drink.

It was very tasty, indeed, Izzy thought: rather like a warm milkshake spiked with rum. Not bad at all.

Then, it was time to make the gift exchange.

Fine writing paper, small leather bound books of poetry or Bible excerpts, and silk ribbons for the ladies; pipe tobacco, ink and fountain pens with extra nibs for the men. Then finally, all the guests departed, leaving the four Sturdevants alone once more.

All the servants had been given the following day, St. Stephen's Day or 'Boxing Day' in England, the day off. Martha and her sister and son had planned to visit Martha's older sister who was married to a farmer and had her own home in Black Walnut Bottom. Because Roger and Belinda knew no one in Braintrim, Martha had very kindly asked if the two servants from Charlottesville would like to accompany them, and so a very jolly party would leave at the crack of the following day's dawn.

Sam had insisted they take his carriage to make the journey, commenting that it would give Martha and her family much more time to visit. Roger and Ephraim had decided to drive the horses together, allowing Martha, Becky and Belinda the luxury of riding within.

But all the servants were now snugly abed, even though it was just after eight in the evening, and so the four Sturdevants gathered in the front parlor to share the rest of the gifts, and a final glass or two of port.

Before Sam could pour out any libations, however, Josh urged a fairly large, heavy package on him, which his twin duly opened. Inside was a generously sized bottle of French brandy that Josh had brought back just a couple of months before from that country.

"Ah, well, now: 'tis sure we shall all have some of this," Sam announced, very pleased, and poured a measure in everyone's glass.

Elizabeth took a sip and coughed in surprise, her eyes watering. "'Tis very strong," she managed, but smiled nonetheless, though she tipped the rest of the brandy in her glass into her husband's.

Sam's other gifts from Josh and Izzy were a brand new, revised Atlas of the World whose hand-colored, oversized pages held maps and accounts of all the countries on the globe, and several new books as well as pipe tobacco from Virginia.

"Oh, such wondrous gifts!" Sam exclaimed, and Josh and Izzy beamed at each other. They had known exactly what to get for Sam.

Elizabeth's gifts were a multi colored, mouth blown glass épergne from Europe by way of London that Josh and Izzy had acquired on their honeymoon and kept with them until they could transport it safely to Elizabeth, and several lengths of the newest brocades and silks in all the most fashionable shades along with an assortment of braids, tassels and trims. Josh had also, at Izzy's behest, brought back a small flacon of French *rose absolue* perfume for his sister in law.

"There's also a length of very fine black wool in with your fabrics," commented Izzy to her delighted sister in law. "And a pattern for a pair of long trousers such as Josh wears, for Sam," she added, a mischievous smile on her face as she caught Sam's eye.

"Aye, tell us about these long trousers, then, brother," Sam urged. But Josh ceded that topic to Izzy, who held forth on the changes in men's fashions for a short while.

"I would not that anyone would think me a Macaroni," Sam said gravely.

Izzy giggled at the term: it was a decade or more out of date. "The current word is 'dandy'" she corrected Sam. "And no one will think that of you. Why, Mr. Jefferson wears long trousers almost exclusively unless he is wearing fancy dress," she added with a confirming nod. "He says 'tis more sober and rational than breeches," she added solemnly, but her eyes twinkled.

The gifts from Sam and Elizabeth to Josh and Izzy were no less fine and given, as had been the others, with much love.

A silver cravat pin and a set of matching cufflinks were Josh's gifts.

"We know your style of dress is of a higher tone in Charlottesville," Sam teased his twin.

But the pin was very fine, and the cufflinks, although plain, represented a new trend in fashion that Izzy was surprised had made it to rural

Pennsylvania. Most men still used buttons to secure the cuffs of their shirts. However, for about half a century, metal button and latch type connectors had been used among the aristocracy, the wealthy and the very fashion conscious, although cufflinks would not be mass produced and commonly used for another fifty or so years. Sam said he'd found the pin and the cufflinks at a jeweler near Tunkhannock, who was also a silversmith and made many of his own designs.

Izzy reflected that, although rural, the area was near enough to the bustling Wyoming Valley and not so far from Philadelphia or even New York that some trends might not be embraced.

Izzy's gift was a wedding ring quilt with their names and the date of their marriage embroidered along the lower edge. It was done in such fine thread as Izzy had rarely seen. Elizabeth said quietly that she had made the quilt herself.

"It looks like needlepoint lace embroidery!" Izzy exclaimed, examining the gift.

Elizabeth admitted that it was, and that Sam had gone through one of his business friends to obtain not only the correct type and weight of silk thread, in the colors Elizabeth wanted, all the way from Brussels.

The quilt's background was ivory, and the interlocking wedding rings that Elizabeth had embroidered were done in a rainbow of pastels, each square holding a differently colored pair.

"Oh this is just wonderful!" Izzy gasped, lifting the quilt and turning it this way and that in the fire and candle lit parlor. "And 'tis all the more beautiful, because you made it, for me," she finished, a catch in her voice.

When everyone decided it was time to go to bed, Sam banked the parlor fire and they tiptoed single file up the staircase to the top floor, carrying candles in brass holders. The stairs creaked, just as they still would in the future, Izzy realized, and bit back a giggle.

At the door to Elizabeth and Sam's bedchamber, the four of them made sign language like motions to say good night, and parted.

Izzy and Josh went the few paces down the hall to the bedchamber they were to use, and tiptoed inside as silently as they could. Both Nicholas and Cordelia were sleeping peacefully in their beds: Cordelia clutching a new, stuffed sewn toy that had been a gift from Elizabeth and Sam, and Nicholas holding tightly to a small wooden flute that had been his gift, whittled by his Uncle himself.

Satisfied that their children were peacefully in dream land, Josh blew out their candle and put the holder on a high shelf.

It wasn't cold in the small bedchamber: the house's huge central chimney kept the heat for hours and radiated it out on the top floor, where there were no fireplaces. Josh reached over to the single window, and partly opened the pretty East Indian printed cotton curtain that covered it. A shaft of wintry moonlight hit the three-quarter rope bed's colorful 'Courthouse Steps' quilt and the two plump pillows dressed in their white muslin cases.

"My stays," whispered Izzy nearly soundlessly, and turned her back to her husband. She had wriggled out of her gown by herself, as it fastened at the side with hooks and eyes; it now hung on one of their friend Thomas Jefferson's new wooden 'hangers,' a dozen of which had been his holiday gift to the couple. Izzy intended to show the hangers she'd brought to use to Elizabeth, and send her some if she liked the concept as much as Izzy did.

Gently, Josh reached out and pulled on the laces fastening his wife's pair of stays; they fell apart loosely, and he engineered the rest with two fingers inserted between her silk chemise and the stays.

Silently, Izzy put the stays on top of the trunk she'd brought, which was now against a wall, then turned back to Josh. Without a word, she divested him of his coat and waistcoat, pulling his stock off and his shirt up and out of his narrow fall trousers. She unbuttoned these as well, and slid his braces over his shoulders, letting the trousers fall to the floor.

"Happy, happy Christmas, my darling wife," Josh murmured into Izzy's hair as she bent to retrieve the trousers and secure them on an empty peg.

She raised her face to his. "Happy Christmas, beloved," she whispered back, and pressed close to him, her thin silk and his fine muslin all that came between them.

They crept as noiselessly as possible into bed, and Josh reached over and drew the curtain closed again, so the room was plunged into darkness.

His breath came warm on her neck, and his kiss was insistent. Barely making a sound, Izzy moved against the sheets until she was beneath him…

There were to be many days of visiting back and forth, beginning on the twenty-seventh. Everyone who had servants, and that was almost all of the families within the Sturdevants' acquaintance, gave the day after Christmas as a holiday. So no visiting was done then, and it was generally a time for families to remain at home and recover from the festivities of the day before.

Izzy knew that they were expected for a dinner party at the Skinners' and a final family dinner at the Reverend and Mrs. Sturdevants' home just before they departed for Charlottesville right after Twelfth Night. In between there would be 'afternoon calls' to nearly every family in Braintrim, the Eddy and Black Walnut, and a couple as far away as Auburn and Wyalusing. Conversely, Elizabeth would hold a number of 'At Home' days so that the friends she and Izzy had visited could return the visits.

There was also, of course, the Christmas Ball, which would take place on December 31st. Although New Year's was not the celebration in the Federalist/ Regency period that it would become in later decades, the fact that this year marked a new century and carried with it all the hope and confidence of a very new Nation, made it quite special. More elaborate observances had therefore been planned.

It was with the happy expectation of all of these delightful events that Izzy snuggled into Josh's arms and drifted off to sleep that Christmas night, feeling more at home and at peace than she had ever felt in her 'own' modern time.

# CHAPTER SIXTEEN

The twenty-sixth was a quiet day: the four Sturdevants and their children relaxed, ate the leftovers from the Christmas Day feasting, and occupied themselves with pursuits that were their own personal pleasures. There would be time enough in the coming days for the concerns of others: today was just for them.

The children, of course, played: many new toys had been among their gifts, as well as material for new clothing, which hadn't interested them much, and some coloring books, which would be saved for another day.

The coloring books, which would properly be invented in the 1880's by the McLoughlin Brothers and Kate Greenaway, had been Izzy's creation. Although she was not consciously a supporter of the democratization of art espoused by painters like Sir Joshua Reynolds, Izzy did believe that children could more easily learn things like hand and eye coordination, spatial judgement skills, the alphabet, shapes, and colors if they had something fun and instructive to teach them.

Therefore, she had obtained a quantity of full sized foolscap paper which she had then folded and inserted one inside the other to make booklets of eight pages each, which she secured with pieces of yarn tied at the top and bottom. On these pages she had drawn the outlines of simple landscapes and still life compositions: a house in a meadow, a forest of pine trees, a bowl of different sorts of fruit, various birds and animals, and the letters of the alphabet. She had been careful to use the alphabet that was currently employed, and included the antique medial 's' that still looked like an 'f' to her.

Obtaining crayons to go with the coloring books, however, proved to be a road block: crayons as Izzy knew them wouldn't be invented for another hundred years. There were 'Conté crayons' or lithographic crayons out of Paris that had been developed alongside the birth of lithography in the early part of the decade. However, these were manufactured in dull shades like graphite, rust and beige: Izzy didn't think children would enjoy using those.

She briefly considered getting some colored chalks, until she realized that these wouldn't adhere to the foolscap very well and would end up smudging. She knew she could get watercolors or oils for the children, but they were too young for such things, and at this time in history, such paints were still toxic.

Izzy finally settled on a selection of grease pencils in black, brown, yellow, red, blue and white. Thomas Jefferson had suggested them to her, after Izzy had confided in him what she had in mind. Made with wax, tallow, and pigments, these thick pencil-shaped tubes contained lead and similar toxic ingredients, so Izzy was certain to make sure each one was securely wrapped with paper so the children wouldn't absorb the lead as they held them. But the grease pencils' colors were bright, and even if they weren't what Izzy'd had as a child, the famous 'box of 64' crayons, they would work.

On the day after Christmas, while the children played, Sam plunged into his new Atlas; Elizabeth, whose father had gifted her with some new sheet music, began to learn the second movement of Beethoven's 'new' *Symphony Pathétique*, or the Eighth Symphony.

Josh kept an eye on the children while he read the new Philadelphia-based Weekly Magazine, containing a novel excerpt called 'Sky Walk' by Benjamin Brockton Brown. Izzy hadn't been familiar with the name, and not for the first time wished she had the internet at her fingertips so she could look him up. However, scanning the excerpt, it seemed to her that Brown was one of the first authors of what would later be called the American Gothic Novel.

For her part, Izzy found herself overcome with an atypical lassitude. She thought perhaps she was still bound by the dreamily romantic mood in which she'd ended the previous night, for she found herself wishing somewhat scandalously that she and Josh could sneak away somehow up to their little bed chamber, unobserved.

However, with just the four adults in the house, such subterfuge would be nearly impossible. So Izzy had to be content to just think her thoughts and admire her husband from afar, and listen to the beautiful notes flowing from Elizabeth's talented fingers.

The Romantic melody suited her sister in law, and Izzy realized anew just how gifted Elizabeth was: her cold reading of the sheet music was very nearly note perfect and the second time through, she gave the music its full expression.

The winter's day was fine and clear, and after a rather catch-as-catch-can late day meal, Josh and Sam went for a ride out towards the eastern edges of the settlement. Sam said he wanted to show Josh a site he had in mind for a future building project.

Elizabeth and Izzy fed and nursed the children and then put them down for their naps; Elizabeth brought out some sewing, and Izzy began to read a book of poetry she'd found on a bookshelf in the River Room, but couldn't concentrate. She found herself just wandering thoughtfully through the rooms of what would always in her mind be 'The Oldest House.'

When Josh and Sam returned, Izzy, still in her peculiar mood, followed her husband upstairs, insisting that he had to change his trousers so the ones he had on—which she said were damp—could dry.

Josh didn't think his trousers were damp at all, but he did as Izzy asked, discovering when she gleefully shut and latched the bed chamber door behind them what her real intentions were. In truth, he was quite glad of the opportunity, and he thought that if they were quick, and very quiet, their afternoon dalliance might not be discovered.

"Do not unlace your stays," Josh whispered to his wife as he quickly undid the narrow fall front of his 'damp' trousers, then guided Izzy towards the patchwork quilt that covered their rope bed. "Just— your skirt and petticoat…" he murmured as he rucked the layers of fabric up around Izzy's hips, then leaned forward to embrace her.

Izzy gasped with pleasure.

In the clear light of the late winter afternoon they spent an extremely enjoyable quarter hour, knowing that the children were still asleep before the Keeping Room fire with Elizabeth and now Sam, on watch.

Languidly, Izzy rolled onto her back, and watched Josh as he put his clothing back on, careful to wear a different pair of trousers; he hung the 'damp' ones on one of Mr Jefferson's hangers.

"Should I bring these downstairs to lay before a fire, or do you think they will dry here?" Josh asked his wife, who regarded him from her position atop the quilt.

"They should dry up here," Izzy replied, stifling a yawn. "Sorry—I'm just so relaxed," she smiled at Josh, and stretched every limb.

"'Tis nice, it being just us," Josh agreed. "I respect and am very fond, indeed, of Belinda and Roger as well as Mariah and Lucy," he said, low, naming the four members of staff in their household. "But 'tis very different not having anyone else about."

Izzy nodded. "Even though we do have our privacy, and even though at home their rooms are nowhere near ours, it's just the sense of having other adults around...yet here, we have Sam and Lizzie, so I don't know why that's different, but it is somehow," she murmured.

Josh gave her a crooked grin. "Perhaps because they seek to snatch some privacy for themselves, just as we do, and are tacitly aware of our attempts."

Izzy smiled. What Josh said was true, and she always tried to ensure that Elizabeth and Sam had some time to alone.

"Well, wife—you are going to stand up and come downstairs eventually, are you not?" he joked, for Izzy was still prone, her printed calico dress rumpled and her cap falling off her coppery curls.

Izzy smiled and sighed. "I guess so," she replied. "Though remaining abed has its charms."

## CHAPTER SEVENTEEN

On the twenty-seventh, Izzy and Elizabeth consulted with Martha over the lengths of material Elizabeth had been given, and the first of several new gowns was planned. Martha said she would start in on the gown that very morning, and with Belinda and Roger here for the next several days, she thought she might have enough time to finish it, since they could help out with some of her regular chores.

Martha also asked Izzy if she could examine one or two of the gowns that she had brought with her.

"They are couture, Madame Sturdevant," Martha explained deferentially. "And I am sure that if I could study the way in which their seams are joined and their designs are worked I could attempt something like it for Mrs. Sturdevant," Martha finished.

Izzy was happy to comply, and told the housekeeper she could look at any garment of hers she wished to.

The ladies were scheduled to make afternoon visits to the Nabbs and the Vaughans, both of whom lived west of Braintrim Village. However, when Elizabeth appeared in the Keeping Room, dressed for the outing in a dark grey wool pelisse and bonnet, she looked quite drawn.

"Lizzie, what is it?" Izzy asked immediately, concerned. "You were fine this morning—are you ill?" she asked with a frown. As a matter of fact, Elizabeth had been all smiles as they had examined the fabrics and designed the new gown.

Elizabeth sighed and shook her head. "No. I am well—enough, Izzy. Thank you." She paused, and then whispered only that her monthly cramps and bleeding had just come upon her.

"Ah, 'tis enough to make anyone feel unwell," sympathized Izzy. Indeed, her own monthlies would likely arrive before they headed back to Charlottesville. Although nursing sometimes held a woman's cycle in abeyance, eventually things returned to their normal course. "Do you wish to stay home? I can make your regrets," she offered.

Elizabeth shook her head and gave a wan smile. "No—'tis not so bad that I cannot go, although I am glad that tomorrow is one of our 'at home' days, as I feel by then I shall most surely wish to remain here."

Izzy nodded. Then she peered into her sister in law's face intently. "Oh, Lizzie—you thought—you were hoping..."

Elizabeth nodded. "It was before the leaves fell that I last bled," she whispered. "And so, I thought... I hoped...Peter will be two years of age in February," she murmured. "And Sam and I have been—" she trailed off and shrugged.

"You'll have another baby, Lizzie, never fear," Izzy reassured her. "But it may take, erm, a little longer than you might wish. Be of good cheer, and be grateful that with luck, both your boys will be weaned before you yet again fall pregnant!" she declared with a smile.

Elizabeth sighed. "Yes, you are right," she agreed in a soft voice.

Upon arriving at the first home, they were told that Mrs. Nabb was not at home; but when they arrived at the Vaughans', they discovered Mrs. Nabb to be there before them.

Mrs. Vaughan welcomed Izzy and Elizabeth and ushered them into her front parlor, a room whose interior wood plank walls had been painted the ubiquitous Colonial aqua-green, and whose wood floor shone with wax and polishing.

Mrs. Vaughan's gate leg table held a tea and coffee service, clearly her pride and joy, and an array of cups and saucers, and plates with savory biscuits, and an impressive plum cake. A female servant with the map of Ireland on her freckled face took everyone's outer wraps, while another brought fresh hot water for the tea.

"I am so thankful you came out to see us!" declared Mrs. Vaughan with a shake of her greying curls: they hung in front of her ears and below her cap and danced as she moved. One of Mrs. Vaughan's blue eyes did not track properly, and when she spoke, Izzy was never sure who was being addressed. Nonetheless, when Mrs. Vaughan invited them to sit and declared herself 'ever so anxious' to hear about goings on in Charlottesville, Izzy was quite sure she was the one in the spotlight.

Obligingly, Izzy gave her audience a run down of what Charlottesville society was like, including her activities, which included shopping and socializing as well as charity work.

Mrs. Vaughan appeared enthralled, nodding and smiling, her grey curls bobbing with osmotic enthusiasm.

Mrs. Nabb listened in stony silence, her gaze flat and emotionless.

Izzy did not know either woman well, having only run into them at the Braintrim church. She had been surprised when Elizabeth had told her that morning as they had perused the fabrics, that they would be their first visits during this holiday period. But her sister in law had merely smiled wryly and said, 'some things it's best to get over with quickly.'

Elizabeth had not minded Mrs. Vaughan, she had said, too much, even if she did think the woman quite silly.

'Still, a good deal of that is because of the time in which she was brought up,' Elizabeth had explained to Izzy. Mrs. Vaughan was now in her seventies, and so had been almost a contemporary of Benjamin Franklin and of Washington. 'The ways things were done when she was young, and the expectations people had for women were very different from today,' Elizabeth had opined.

Izzy had bitten her lip and thought, oh, Elizabeth, if you only knew just how different all of that would become over time!

"And how is your household?" Mrs. Nabb inquired now in a tone that suggested she expected a negative reply. Her brownish-grey hair was pulled severely back under a plain cap, for she did not bother much with her appearance, and her dark eyes were as sharp as the lines etched into her jowly face.

Mrs. Nabb fretted a great deal, and made mockery of the saying that fat people were jolly, for she was of a largely melancholy disposition: dissatisfied with her own life, she was determined to do what she could to bring others down to her level.

Izzy spoke then, smilingly, of Nicholas and Cordelia, their friends, and Josh's work, although the latter held very little detail.

The Irish-faced servant brought in a fresh pitcher of milk for their tea, spilling a little over the rim as she placed it on the table.

Mrs. Vaughan didn't seem to notice, or if she did, she didn't care.

Mrs. Nabb tut-tutted behind her handkerchief.

"Did you find it difficult, in Charlottesville, to find good servants?" Mrs. Nabb asked loudly as the servant, having overheard the visitor, fairly ran out of the room, her face bright red with embarrassment.

Mrs. Nabb accepted a cup of tea from Mrs. Vaughan and sat back, smoothing the skirt of her mud green wool dress that was out of fashion by several years.

Although older women such as Mrs. Nabb and Mrs. Vaughan tended to favor the lower waistline and stronger corseting of the late 1700 fashions, Izzy had noticed with approval that their hostess sported a high waisted dress in a deep crimson wool, accented with brown velvet ribbon. Mrs. Nabb, apparently, preferred the natural waistline dress and probably would wear those for the next three decades until they became fashionable again. If she lived that long.

Izzy shook her head and explained they way in which they had found their household staff, and the fact that they were all from the same island in the West Indies. Then she mentioned that she and Josh had freed them as soon as they had been bought.

"But do you not find that troublesome?" queried Mrs. Nabb, looking dubious.

"Oh, do have some plum cake," Mrs. Vaughan broke in anxiously: her smile was nervous, possibly because she knew where Mrs. Nabb was going with her topic of conversation.

Izzy smiled at her hostess. "I should love some, thank you," she said. Then she turned back to Mrs. Nabb, and shook her head. "Not at all troublesome—in what way do you mean?" she queried. "That they are all from the same village, or that they are free?" she asked innocently, yet her question brought the hidden agenda straight out into the light so everyone could see it.

Mrs. Vaughan handed Izzy a large slice of cake, then served Elizabeth, who asked for a smaller piece.

Mrs. Nabb began to talk about the continuing slave revolts in Saint Domingue, owned by France, which had started nearly a decade before. Her opinion seemed to be that the slaves should concentrate on doing their jobs, and that by revolting they were trying to upset the world's economy.

Izzy nearly choked on her plum cake at that declaration, but then recalled that France and England were, at the moment, the two 'super powers' in the western world, so those countries' economies were of great importance; the Orient, just now, was largely unknown and in any case discounted except as a source of silk, spice and opium although the vastly different beauty of its landscapes and people had begun to fascinate artists. Within a half century, Orientalia would infiltrate sophisticated taste in every aspect of society, and by the late Victorian period it would be an absolute obsession.

Nonetheless, it would never have dawned to most people in the U.S. in 1799 that China, Japan and India would in time become forces in their own right to be reckoned with.

As for the slaves' revolt's impact on the 'world economy,' sugar plantations in the Caribbean had become essential to European and North American life and cuisine; additionally, coffee, cocoa, cotton and dyes were also exported from there to Europe and North America.

The Caucasian planters on the islands employed black slaves brought over from Africa to work the extensive plantations, but treatment of them and conditions in which they lived and worked were poor. There was an abundance of slaves, too, which meant that when one died, it was easy to replace him or her. This led to the continuing devaluation of their lives, and an ongoing marginalization of their humanity.

By 1789, the slaves in the Caribbean had out-numbered their masters ten to one and, led by Toussaint L'Ouverture, began a series of revolts that had been inspired by the French Revolution and the Enlightenment.

# CHAPTER EIGHTEEN

"Why, that they are free, Mrs. Sturdevant!" Mrs. Nabb replied now in a tone of voice suggesting that Izzy should have known that. She shook her capped head and her jowls waggled beneath the lappets. "'Tis bad enough there are slaves trying to overthrow the state of things and be free down in the Islands," she continued, clacking her tongue again. "And that L'Overture man whipping them all into a frenzy..."

Mrs. Nabb accepted a piece of cake from her hostess which, if she had not, Izzy thought Mrs. Vaughan would have tipped into Mrs. Nabb's lap, so eager was she to break the course of the conversation.

"They call him Napoleon-Noir," noted Elizabeth quietly. She took a bite of cake, and smiled: delicious.

"And he is no less militant in his ways than the Little General," Mrs. Nabb rejoined with spirit, using the slightly pejorative nickname for the French leader. She took a large bite of her cake, and chewed vigorously.

Izzy was reminded of the Sturdevants' cow, Sunflower.

"But I ask you:" Mrs. Nabb went on once she had swallowed, "what possible good can his call to revolution do? What can being independent do for those people?" she asked. She sipped at her tea. "Oh, more sugar, please, Mrs. Vaughan, if you would, dear," she murmured, and held out her cup.

Mrs. Vaughan obligingly plopped two more light brown cubes into her guest's cup, and Mrs. Nabb picked up her teaspoon and stirred.

Izzy put her teacup down and cleared her throat.

Elizabeth gave her sister in law a faintly alarmed look: Izzy's color was high and her eyes were very bright.

"What good can independence be to anyone?" Izzy asked in a deceptively innocent voice, but she fixed Mrs. Nabb with a direct stare.

"Well, I mean—those people," repeated Mrs. Nabb in an uncertain tone: Izzy looked rather fierce, and although Mrs. Nabb was quite sure her convictions were correct, something in the French woman's eyes made her begin to doubt herself, just a little. "They are not really, well, capable, are they? I mean, of governing themselves," Mrs. Nabb offered. She took another bite of cake.

"Not capable?" Izzy echoed faintly. She knew that attitudes towards the various races were vastly different now, on the cusp of the 19th century, than they would be in her own time. She had been fortunate that the Sturdevants were by and large relatively liberal when it came to the subject, and although she'd encountered more prejudice in Charlottesville, she had expected it, since it was in the South.

To uncover it here, however, and to hear a woman like Mrs. Nabb so glibly dismiss an entire race as 'incapable' purely because she had heard or been told that opinion, was like a slap in the face.

"Yes—they are like children, really," Mrs. Nabb continued in an entreatingly sweet tone, as though trying to coax Izzy to see her point.

"Are they?" Izzy queried, her voice still mild.

There was silence.

Mrs. Nabb clearly had no idea how to answer that question, and Mrs. Vaughan and Elizabeth knew it had not been meant for them.

"Have you ever known a black slave?" Izzy continued in the silence, endeavoring to make her voice curious, not challenging, although challenging was what she felt.

At the unusual turn of phrase, everyone's eyes swiveled to her.

"People of color," Izzy amended. This only made everyone look perplexedly at each other, although Elizabeth knew what her sister in law meant.

"My servants are white," admitted Mrs. Vaughan, sounding almost guilty.

Mrs. Nabb nodded wordlessly.

"Well, then, perhaps judging an entire population when you have never known even a one, is not the best, erm, course," Izzy offered, modifying her tone as she spoke so that by the end of her comment, her voice had returned to the normal range—for it had started out quite sharp.

"Martha is freed, as is her son, Ephraim," Elizabeth put in quietly. "And Martha reads and writes, does sums, and has taught Ephraim the same."

Izzy knew it wouldn't be until towards the middle of the next century that black universities began; until then, people of color in the fledgeling United States had to obtain what education they could any way they could. "He's very intelligent," Izzy said, then, of Ephraim. "We also made certain that all of our staff—" she intentionally did not use the word 'servant'—"can read and write, both French and English," she added mildly.

"But my dear! What a waste of effort!" Mrs. Nabb exclaimed, putting her tea cup and saucer down on a small table at her side and leaning forward, as if to impress her point of view on Izzy by her nearness.

"How do you mean? Being able to read and write enables our staff to conduct the business of the household properly, and ensures that they—and by extension we—will not be taken advantage of," Izzy returned with spirit.

"But—but teaching people like that to read, and to figure sums! It will do nothing for them but give them ideas above their station," she finished sourly.

"Their station?" Izzy echoed disbelieving. "Their station is that of humanity, Mrs. Nabb, and of working at honest employment and of finding what joy they may in life. For does not our Constitution declare that everyone has the right to freedom and the pursuit of happiness?" she challenged.

"Why, yes, of course— but the Constitution was not referring to those people," she insisted.

The next words out of Izzy's mouth were going to be, 'How do *you* know what the intent of the Constitution is and what makes you worthy to interpret it?' for she had framed the riposte in her mind. But luckily for the convention of the afternoon visit, Elizabeth interrupted with a comment she hoped would divert the conversation a little bit.

"Mr. Sturdevant has taken Ephraim on as an apprentice, at the mill," Elizabeth said with a nod and a smile, almost as though the debate of 'station' between Izzy and Mrs. Nabb had not occurred.

"Oh, is that so?" Mrs. Vaughan chimed in, looking grateful. "What a wonderful opportunity for him."

"Indeed, and he is doing very well...Mr. Sturdevant says the boy will likely be running it by the time he is a young man."

Mrs. Nabb looked shocked at this revelation.

Mrs. Vaughan lifted the tea pot and shook it gently to distribute the brewed liquid preparatory to pouring it out.

"Surely not—a person like that? Running a business?" Mrs. Nabb breathed, glaring at Elizabeth. "Do you and Mr. Sturdevant not fear loss of custom?" she asked, sounding genuinely concerned.

Izzy spoke up. "Mrs. Nabb: if you knew that your lumber would be sawn properly and for a reasonable price, why would you not patronize the Sturdevant mill?" she queried. "Surely the fact that it may be run by a Freedman would not influence you, any more than it would affect the quality of the product."

The woman looked uncomfortable.

"Perhaps this boy Ephraim is an unusual example," murmured Mrs. Vaughan in a mollifying voice. Another nervous smile: somehow, she had to pull this conversation back into calmer waters. "More tea?" she asked brightly.

Both Izzy and Elizabeth accepted, and Izzy grabbed a savory biscuit. The plum cake had been delicious, but the biscuits had cheese and herbs and were light and buttery, even without butter.

Izzy discovered she was ravenous, although she'd eaten a very big breakfast. Martha had returned, and in top form had made a platter of griddle cakes, bacon, baked eggs and all manner of other goodies that morning as if to announce that she had resumed her duties, and had the family missed her?

"I do not wish to continue such a divisive discussion," Izzy said suddenly: the stricken face of Mrs. Vaughan as she had poured Mrs. Nabb's second cup of tea and added four sugar cubes had made her realize the effect her commentary was having on what was supposed to be a pleasant social occasion. "But let me just say that I do not suppose that the people of Sainte Domingue would stage a revolt only to run their country's economy into the ground," she announced, and paused.

No one said a word.

"Indeed, Monsieur L'Overture is quite the strategist, both in warfare and in government,  as you yourself pointed out, Mrs. Nabb," she said, tossing her adversary a bone. "I suspect that his guiding hand will enable the revolutionaries, if they are successful, to continue to operate their brisk trade.

You will still have sugar for your tea and cocoa before bed," she added with a smile that belied her inner feelings.

"Well, yes, but perhaps they will raise their prices, to make a greater profit," suggested Mrs. Nabb, looking suddenly alarmed and in any case being unwilling to concede completely despite Izzy's attempts to make peace. "The prices will go sky high!" Mrs. Nabb declared in an rising tone of panic. "No, no, we must not aid Napoleon Noir in his efforts to overthrow the way things are done now," she insisted flatly.

"But you cannot deny an entire segment of the population the right to self government and autonomy merely because of the color of their skin!" insisted Izzy with spirit. She put her teacup down with an audible noise.

Hang pleasant social occasions.

"It is not right. And it is not Christian!" Izzy tossed at Mrs. Nabb, knowing that the last statement would resonate with her.

Mrs. Nabb prided herself, she knew, on being 'a pillar of the church,' and was very active in Reverend Sturdevant's congregation. In truth, that was another reason that Elizabeth had singled Mrs. Nabb out to be the first person they visited during this Season: had she not, she would have heard about it.

"What about what Paul says in Ephesians six?" Mrs. Nabb challenged, predictably. " 'Servants, be obedient to them that are your masters...' surely that is an approbation of slavery?" she asked.

"Why, no, Mrs. Vaughan, I do not believe that to be so," Elizabeth put in mildly. "It is merely an acknowledgement of the fact that slavery existed at that time."

Her sister in law's comment had given Izzy time to think. Although she had never been especially religious and certainly not a Bible-reader, marriage to the son of a minister had made her more conversant with 'the good book.'

"Does not Exodus tell us that anyone who kidnaps someone and sells him or enslaves him, must himself be put to death?" Izzy asked then. She couldn't quote chapter and verse, but her question was rhetorical: of course that's what Exodus said, and they all knew it.

"Oh, yes, but that was back in those times, my dear Mrs. Sturdevant," rejoined Mrs. Nabb with quite a bit of spirit. "Today..."

"Today we should remember that the Bible is as relevant now as it was when it was written," Elizabeth put in, her voice firm and strong. "And we should perhaps recall and be mindful of what Paul tells us in Galatians." She paused, but no one spoke. 'There is neither Jew nor Greek, there is neither slave nor free man, there is neither male nor female; for you are all one in Christ Jesus.'" Elizabeth let her words reverberate in the sitting room. "If that is not a call for unity and equality, I do not know what might be."

## CHAPTER NINETEEN

That evening, Izzy and Elizabeth recounted the unusually lively visit they had had that afternoon at the Vaughans'.

"I suspect Mrs. Nabb thought you would agree with her point of view," offered Sam, having heard his wife and sister in law through. "Quite possibly she was looking forward to an afternoon of head wagging and deploring the state of the world!" he added with a chuckle, trying to lighten the mood. His wife, in particular, seemed especially downcast.

"In Pennsylvania, there are folk who are quite openly abolitionists," Josh began calmly. "As well as people who keep slaves and see no reason not to." He paused. "Here in Braintrim, and the surrounding areas, many of the settlers are from Connecticut and other parts of New England," Josh continued. "They seem to be of a more abolitionist bent, than, say, those who reside in and are from Virginia."

"Yes, as we told you, where we live, freeing your slaves is done, but rarely, and surely not done as we did, almost the moment we purchased them!" Izzy put in with spirit. "If it is done at all, it's done as a reward, for years of service," she added, shaking her head.

"Mrs. Vaughan is from out Wyalusing way," Elizabeth offered.

"What about Mrs. Nabb?" Josh asked, curious.

"I know not about Mrs. Nabb, but Mr. John Nabb is from Towson, very near Baltimore," Sam answered.

"Oh, then it makes a bit more sense that she would be prejudiced," Izzy commented.

"I'll wager you gave her a lot to think on," Josh offered, smiling.

Elizabeth managed a smile and gave a small chuckle. "That we did, Josh, we did," she said with a conspiratorial look at Izzy.

They had gathered in the Keeping Room, where the fire was blazing and the room was cozy and warm.

"I cannot blame the slaves for wanting freedom, and self government, for I hear they are treated very ill," Sam said of the Caribbean slaves.

"I would not be surprised if those enslaved in this country follow in their Caribbean brothers' footsteps," Josh offered. He knew, from discussions he'd had with Izzy when they had freed their own staff, that within a half century that was precisely what would happen. "While there are some who free their slaves and others who do not but who yet treat them very well, there are many who are as bad as the slaveholders in the Indies," he noted with a downturned mouth.

Everyone nodded gravely.

Seeking to lighten the mood, Izzy then asked if anyone wanted to join her in a game of 'Shut the Box,' and the evening progressed on a happier plane.

Sam retrieved the game from a shelf and Josh made everyone a hot toddy with rum and butter blended, then heated by a fire poker. It was not too different from the 'flips' that they'd all enjoyed on Christmas, and as the evening had turned sharply chilly with a cold north wind, the hot drinks were welcome.

"'Twill snow before dawn," Sam presaged close to ten p.m., when they all decided it was time to head up to bed. Elizabeth had already gone up. Now, her husband peered out the window next to the house's wide wood-planked front door.

Izzy crowded next to him and cocked her head so she could see the sky. Clouds covered any stars or moon, so she thought Sam was probably right. Oh well, they were 'at home' the following day, so a little snow wouldn't bother them although it might mean fewer visitors and thus less entertainment. Although, Izzy thought to herself, she might wish to steer clear of the subject of slavery—Caribbean or otherwise—in social settings from now on.

As Sam wavering candle mounted the second set of stairs towards the top floor bed chambers, Josh held Izzy back with a gentle hand. He pointed to the mistletoe ball, hanging in the doorway between the dining room and the stairwell.

By the light of their candle, Izzy could see his dark blue eyes shining; he was smiling, and the dimple on his right cheek showed in the shadows thrown by the flickering flame.

"Wife…" he whispered, drawing her close into an embrace.

"Husband," Izzy murmured against his lips, and kissed him.

They heard the door to Sam and Elizabeth's bedroom close gently above them as their embrace intensified. Then they hastened up the stairs as quickly and quietly as they could, and tiptoed down the hall to their own small bed chamber.


The following day they woke to two inches of fresh snow and a clearing but very cold indigo sky. A brisk north wind still blew, and Martha's hearty breakfast of porridge studded with nuts and dried fruit was very welcome.

The children, of course, wanted to go out and play in the white stuff, and while Elizabeth was concerned that it was too cold for them, Izzy pointed out that the sun was shining and that if they stayed on the south side of the house, there would be little wind. She also said they wouldn't spend a long time outside.

So Elizabeth agreed, and Izzy dressed warmly in her oldest dress, several petticoats, thick stockings, stout boots, and a warm scarf and cape. Then she helped John, Peter and Nicholas dress and put on their knitted mittens and hats, and led them outside.

The snow was of the wrong consistency, light and fluffy, for making a snowman. And in any case, there was not enough of it. However, Izzy showed the boys how to make 'snow angels' and soon, many peculiarly shaped declivities decorated the Sturdevant yard.

"Do you think the river is frozen?" Izzy asked Josh as she brought the three little boys, rosy cheeked and runny-nosed, back into the Keeping Room. Belinda and Becky took the children in hand and Josh helped his wife off with her cloak and scarf.

"Mayhap," Josh answered, giving his wife a critical look. "Why?"

Izzy shrugged. "I just thought it might be fun to walk on it, if it is. I know we don't have ice skates, but we could walk on it...I've never walked across a river," she added, sounding appealingly forlorn.

Josh sighed. "If it stays this cold, and Sam says he thinks it will, we can test it near the bank, but 'tis rare for the river to freeze completely," he added. Then: "there is, of course, the Spring Hill Pond," he said.

Izzy, who didn't know what pond he meant, just looked at him.

"'Tis a popular place for ice skating, and sometimes there is a toboggan one may ride, as well..." Josh informed her with a tempting smile. "Did you never go there during the year you spent here?" he inquired, curious.

"No—never!" Izzy replied. Then: "I suspect I was pre-occupied with Lizzie's lying in," she murmured, recalling those months.

"Well, 'tis quite a fine pond, and the Tewksbury boys, whose property the pond is on, keep the surface clear of snow..." Josh continued.

"Ooooh! Can we go? Can we? Please? The boys would love it," she said as an added inducement, and Josh laughed.

"Indeed they would," he agreed, and explained that when he and Sam had been little, their mother had taken them and any other children who were old enough, to this pond to skate and otherwise amuse themselves. "If we get more snow, there is also a fine sledding hill nearby," Josh finished as he and Izzy started for the stairs.

"That sounds perfect!" Izzy exclaimed, grabbing an apple from the bowl on the table, and beginning to munch it as they went.

"Playing in the snow has given you an appetite," Josh commented with a loving glance.

Izzy nodded. "Yes, and it'll be a long afternoon of visits before dinner," she moaned with a grin, and headed up to the top floor to change and freshen up for their 'at home.'

Mrs. Vaughan and Mrs. Nabb were the first to arrive at the Sturdevants' for their 'at home' that afternoon. Clearly, the latter had collected the former in her barouche, and so they arrived together, and in quite grand style. Becky brought the two ladies up from the Keeping Room where she had taken their outer garments to hang up, and ushered them into what Izzy still called the 'River Room.'

Although there was, of course, the front parlor, there were usually so many visitors during an 'at home' that even though each visitor didn't stay very long, the more intimate parlor could get quite crowded. So Elizabeth had taken to holding her 'at homes' in the larger River Room. The pianoforte was there, as well, and ample light from the large windows meant that anything printed that might be shared or read aloud, and any stitchery that might be worked would be easily seen.

"How are you feeling?" Izzy asked in a concerned tone as she entered the River Room to find her sister in law seated on the upholstered settee, her ever present needlework to hand. Elizabeth had chosen her dark maroon and black patterned calico dress with the fashionable high waist accented with a small belt. She wore her second best lace cap, and a cameo Izzy knew had been her grandmother's at her throat.

Elizabeth smiled. "'Tis painful, but the willow bark tea eases the worst of it," she replied.

Izzy nodded as she took her spot in a comfortable armchair and picked up a small book of verse. Mrs. Vaughan and Mrs. Nabb had just pulled up to the front door, and Izzy wanted to look busy doing something when they arrived.

'I should be reading *Uncle Tom's Cabin*,' she thought to herself with a smirk. But of course, that book hadn't been written yet.

She gazed down at her pale pink silk gown, embroidered in a pattern of small apples and blossoms, and trimmed with braiding in a deep rose. She gave a tug to her own double ruffle cap. Her hair had corkscrewed wildly after her romp in the snow with the children, and she had had a difficult time combing the snarls out of it, and then corralling it into an ersatz French twist before popping her cap atop it.

The two ladies were heard tromping up the stairs moments later and both Izzy and Elizabeth looked towards the doorway, pleasant expressions on their faces.

Becky announced the ladies, who then sailed into the room as though no disagreement had been part of the previous day's visit whatsoever.

It was fortunate that Mrs. Vaughan and Mrs. Nabb did not stay too long: just long enough for a quick cup of tea and a biscuit—in Mrs. Nabb's case, three—and then they left. It was likely they had other visits to make, but it may also have been the arrival of Mrs. Goldner to the Sturdevants' 'at home' which precipitated at least Mrs. Nabb's departure.

The day before, when Izzy and Elizabeth had been taking their leave once the slavery debacle had ended, they had mentioned that their next stop was the Goldner farm. At this, Mrs. Nabb's look had turned very sour. Poor Mrs. Vaughan had said nothing, but had shot her guests entreating looks, and no more had been said on the subject.

En route to the Goldners' home, which was not far from Mrs. Vaughan's, Izzy had asked Elizabeth about it.

'Of course, you remember Thomas Goldner,' Elizabeth had begun, her voice low as the carriage had swayed gently over the hard packed road.

Izzy had nodded: just after her wedding three years before, the small community of Braintrim Village had been rocked by the apparent suicide of one of the Clooney children, a teenaged girl. Izzy had been instrumental in proving that the child had not died by her own hand, but had been murdered, and Thomas Goldner, it turned out, had been uncovered as the murderer. He had killed himself shortly after being charged, and when Izzy and Josh had left on their honeymoon, there had been some question as to what would become of Goldner's widow and children.

'Yes, you told me that after she sold her half interest in the mill, Mrs. Goldner decided to stay on after all, and work the farm as before, with her children,' Izzy had replied. 'Nathaniel, the oldest boy, is working part time in Sam's mill, isn't he?' she had asked, then.

Elizabeth had nodded. 'Indeed, and doing very well. Now that Sam has the second mill, he relies on Nathaniel to run the original one,' she had added, sounding proud of her husband's business acumen. 'He and Ephraim make a wonderful team, and Sam is so delighted...' Elizabeth had paused. 'Mrs. Goldner got a very fair price for her share of the mill. She and her oldest daughter have started rather a successful sheep farming enterprise—you remember it?' she had asked, and Izzy had nodded: she remembered the farm well. 'They hire a shearer, then they spin the wool into yarn, dye it, and sell it,' Elizabeth had told her as that very farm had come into sight over the hill. 'Some is in the draper's in the village, and I heard just a fortnight ago that the large draper's in Tunkhannock wants to stock it!' Elizabeth had finished.

From information they had exchanged in their letters during the past three years, Izzy had known that Mrs. Goldner, who had feared being ostracized because of her husband's crimes and had once planned to relocate, had decided to remain in Braintrim, and face down detractors and nay sayers. Mrs. Nabb, obviously, was one of these who had decided that she could not associate with Mrs. Goldner or see her socially. Elizabeth had never mentioned any social situations where Mrs. Goldner had been snubbed, so Izzy had concluded that only a few people in Braintrim had chosen to strike the Goldner name from their list of friends.

Now, as the sound of their first visitors' barouche rolling away echoed up through the River Room windows, the tap tapping of Elvira and Caroline Goldners' booted feet following Becky up the stairs could be heard.

"I do hope Mrs. Nabb didn't do herself a mischief leaping into her barouche!" Izzy said, *sotto voce,* and with a wicked grin.

Elizabeth let out a giggly peal of laughter and turned a smiling face to the two Goldner women.

"Well, you are very merry!" Elvira Goldner said, looking pleased, and hastening over to Elizabeth to give her a kiss on the cheek.

In the interval right after the scandal involving her husband, Elvira had discovered that Sam and

Elizabeth Sturdevant were as friendly and loyal to her as they had ever been. Although they never made an occasion out of it, the Sturdevants had made a point of inviting the widow and her children for dinner at least once a week, and of sending over 'extra' breads or cuts of meat.

Additionally, of course, Sam had hired Nathaniel the following year when the boy had finished his schooling, and at the holidays, Elizabeth and Sam had always managed to deliver attractive, useful things to the Goldners, be it special food, material for new clothing or hand-carved toys for the little ones.

Elvira had never forgotten these small kindnesses, and so kissed Elizabeth in greeting, and gazed on her fondly. She was well aware of the way a few in the community regarded her and her family, and the way she had been treated by Mrs. Nabb and others of her ilk. Therefore, Elizabeth and Sam's continued friendship was very precious to her.

Elvira and Caroline wore plain dresses in the same high-waisted style: Caroline's a pretty blue calico with small pastel flowers, and Elvira's a rich chocolate brown solid. Both sported beautifully woven shawls of their own making: Caroline's in a rainbow of pastel yarns that highlighted the pastel flowers in her dress, and her mother's in shades of deep gold.

After the usual opening exchanges, Izzy had to reach out and touch Caroline's shawl.

"It's so soft!" she exclaimed in surprise. She had expected wool to have a sturdier feel, but this was like gossamer in her hand. "And how did you get it to do that, with the colors, go from one to another?" she asked, curious, as she examined an edge of the shawl minutely.

Caroline smiled and replied that the shawls were a new endeavor, and something she herself had thought of and developed. "We have not made any yet, to sell," she told her. "Indeed, I do believe that this is the first we have worn them!"

"Our wool is among the softest you will find," Elvira told Izzy proudly, and explained the several extra steps she and her daughter took to ensure this.

"I see," Izzy noted. "And the colors?" she asked again.

Caroline explained that the pastel colors were obtained by first dyeing the entire skein of wool a pale pink. Then the skein was twisted and folded, then dip-dyed into pigment baths of other colors, like indigo blue, red, and yellow. The result was that the finished yarn was pink, red, yellow, and bluish-purple, the colors appearing somewhat randomly along the yarn.

For the gold-toned shawl, the yarn had first been dyed pale yellow, then twisted and folded and dip-dyed in progressively darker treatments of gold dye until the yarn was randomly colored in all the sunny tones from end to end.

Garments knitted or woven from yarn dyed in this manner took on a muted patchwork kind of pattern with the colors seeming to flow, one into the next. In addition to their knitting needles, Elvira and Caroline had just invested in a small loom, and it had been on this that Caroline's shawl had been woven.

"It is astoundingly beautiful!" Izzy breathed. She had not seen the like anywhere, and gave Elvira's shawl a long look, too. "Might I ask that you make a shawl—like Caroline's—for me? Whilst I am here?" she asked eagerly.

"Why certainly, Mrs. Sturdevant, we should be delighted!" Elvira declared immediately. She was a bit surprised, because Izzy's clothing was clearly couturier, not home-made, and although it was in the same basic style that they all wore, the finishing and trim work set it above the rest. Elvira was surprised, and very pleased, that Izzy would wear one of their own hand woven shawls with her beautifully fine clothes.

When Izzy asked the price, Elvira insisted that the shawl would be a gift, but Izzy then explained her ulterior motive.

"I do wish to own such a lovely thing for myself," she told the Goldners. "But—I have never seen a woven garment dyed in such a fashion. And I think it would be extremely popular in Virginia—and in Washington, as well," she explained. "I'd like to wear your shawl to show people of my acquaintance what you can do," she continued. "So they may write to you and purchase similar shawls for themselves," she finished.

Elvira and Caroline at first looked dumbfounded and then delighted.

"And I'll also show the shawl to my tailor and the draper's shop that's just opened on the square in Charlottesville," Izzy continued. "I'll wager they will both be interested in your wools: the tailor to use to make bespoke gowns and coats and so on, and the draper to sell."

"Oh, I cannot imagine how lovely an entire gown made of our dyed and tied wool might be!" Caroline exclaimed, her eyes shining.

Elizabeth looked over at her sister in law and gave her a sweet smile.

It was true that the Goldners had got on a much more firm economic footing in the past year or so, with Nathaniel steadily employed and the sheep farm and wool business established. But sales further afield than Braintrim Village or indeed, Luzerne

County, could mean a real windfall to the widow and her family.

"In that case, Mrs. Sturdevant, you absolutely must accept the shawl as a gift," Elvira insisted. "And before you leave to return to Virginia, we shall have at least one more for you to take with you, either to give as a gift to a friend, or to show to people you think might be interested in our wools!" she declared.

Izzy reluctantly agreed, still wanting to pay for her shawl, but Elvira was clearly not having any of that.

"I apologize for discussing business, sister," Izzy murmured, low, to Elizabeth. Topics for 'at home' visits were generally the weather, one's health in decorous detail, and occasionally goings on in the village. The previous day's discussion on slavery had been a real departure, and Izzy had apologized to Mrs. Vaughan, too.

"'Tis no matter, I am glad to think you might introduce the Goldners' weaving to the wider world," Elizabeth commented happily now.

As she had done with the first visitors, Becky had presented a tray with tea, small sandwiches and cakes on it, and Elvira, Caroline, Izzy and Elizabeth all munched and sipped as their conversation turned to lighter subjects.

Caroline was 'walking out' with a young man of whom Elvira very much approved, so they gently teased the young woman about her 'beau' and talked of weddings and babies. A half hour flew by, for the four women truly found themselves especially congenial. Then they heard the sound of carriage wheels on the flagstones of the front patio, and Elvira and Caroline stood to take their leave.

# CHAPTER TWENTY ONE

"A successful 'at home,' then?" Sam asked his wife later that afternoon. The men had gone down to Ebenezer Skinner's tavern for the afternoon to do their own 'visiting' with fellow businessmen over a couple of pints of ale, and of course Belinda had seen to the children so that Elizabeth and Izzy could have a pleasant afternoon of visiting with their friends.

Elizabeth nodded, and filled her husband in on just who had stopped by and what had been discussed. Following Elvira and Caroline Goldner's departure, the Laceys, the Chapmans and the Bunnells had all visited, which meant a full schedule of return visits for Elizabeth and Izzy the next day.

When Elizabeth told him about Izzy and her fascination with the shawls, Sam was delighted by Izzy's idea to promote the Goldners' creations in Charlottesville.

"You seem more cheered," Sam said quietly, then. It was just before dinner time, and he had come up to their bedchamber to freshen up. He had found his wife dressed and ready for dinner, but sitting up on their bed, both pillows behind her. "But why are you abed?" he asked, concerned.

Elizabeth had told him, then, and Sam had instantly realized that this had been the cause of Elizabeth's somber mood the last two days.

"We shall keep on trying, Elizabeth," Sam reassured her. "And we shall keep asking God to bless us with a daughter," he added, for he knew how much Elizabeth longed for a little girl.

"Izzy seems sure we shall have more children," Elizabeth murmured.

Sam gave her an odd look, but just nodded, since he knew that their sister in law did occasionally predict something that would in time come true.

"Our visitors are all quite delighted to talk to Izzy," Elizabeth said, then, returning to the topic of their afternoon visits. "She is the exotic drawing card from the far away land of Virginia," she declared, her tone both wry and merry. She laughed.

"'Twas the same at the tavern!" Sam agreed. "Everyone wanted to talk to Joshua, have his opinion, and hear the news from Virginia." He chuckled. "It was quite a respite for me, and a refreshing change."

Normally, anyone Sam met up with at the tavern wanted to bend his ear about business in the region, so he'd been happy to have his twin the cynosure that afternoon, and have a bit of peace for himself.

"Did they ask about his time in France?" Elizabeth asked obliquely of the men at the tavern.

Sam frowned. "Of course. And Joshua told them, less than he told me, of course, and nothing, really, but generalities. Still," he sighed. "They all seemed very happy."

Elizabeth fixed her husband with a pointed look. "Do you not think there was something, well, something *else* Josh was doing over in France?" she asked in a whisper. The very man they spoke of, and his wife, were just in the next bedchamber, themselves readying for dinner. Elizabeth did not wish to be overheard speculating on things she had not been made privy to.

"Something else?" Sam parroted, frowning. "Like what?" But his voice was a whisper, too.

Elizabeth shrugged. "I know he was Mr. Marshall's aide," she began slowly. "And he told us about how handy it was that he speaks French. But I wonder why Josh would have wanted to go? I mean, he was just a secretary, really, and on a trip that was unsuccessful in many respects. Why would he go? And why would Mr. Jefferson let him go? I thought Josh worked very closely with Mr. Jefferson, so I cannot understand why he would want one of his key people gone for weeks and months?" She tipped her head to one side and looked at her husband.

Sam nodded. "'Tis true, what you say, and since Mr. Marshall is one of Mr. Jefferson's chief opponents, it must not have been easy to get Josh included in the delegation." His twin had not confided any more specifics to him than what

Elizabeth had just spoken of. But he, too, had wondered, because he knew his twin, and the gambit just hadn't seemed like something he would want to do. Plus, whenever he spoke of the Marshall delegation to France, Josh's tone and manner became strained: Sam thought there was something more, something his twin wasn't revealing. "Perhaps Mr. Jefferson *wanted* Josh to go with Marshall," Sam suggested now.

Elizabeth thought for a moment. "Izzy says that Mr. Jefferson trusts Joshua completely. And he is very close to her, as well," she added with a confirming nod. "Apparently, Mr. Jefferson thinks of Izzy like a niece and of Josh rather like a son."

"Mmmmm..." Sam thought for a moment as he changed his neck cloth and ran a cool piece of toweling over his face. Then he took his hair out of its tie lacing, combed it, and re-tied it. Here in Braintrim Village, few people wore wigs, except the Judge when he was on his bench. But they still followed the older Colonial fashion of small pony tails for men although cropped hair such as Josh sported was beginning to catch on as a fashion.

"It was, as I said, not a very successful mission," Elizabeth repeated. "And the way President Adams dealt with making the dispatches public, after first trying to keep them a secret...I wonder who gave him that idea? Or the idea to redact the French envoys' names?" she mused, shaking her head.

Even when it had happened and news had spread to Braintrim of what had been done, it had seemed to Elizabeth a very peculiar thing to do. The aftermath of President Adams at first telling the American public that the missives were 'classified,' and then releasing them with the French emissaries' names blanked out, was that he had been ridiculed for his action. The whole thing had thrown doubt on his presidency: if he was trying to keep secrets, should he be President?

"Josh said that President Adams is adamant about not wanting war with France, and he is afraid."

"Our President should not be afraid," Sam rejoined solemnly.

"Izzy and Josh said that was why President Adams tried to keep the missives secret and the envoys' identities unknown—he didn't want to further anger the French," Elizabeth offered.

Sam admitted that he had heard that, too, from other people, but had always found it a very thin excuse.

Elizabeth nodded her agreement. "Then… if the President did not act as he did of his own volition, the only reasonable explanation is that someone convinced him to act in that fashion," she said slowly, "and to use fear of further angering the French as an excuse." She paused. "Mayhap that encouragement was made, knowing that such actions would discredit the President in the eyes of the people?" she ventured.

Sam slid a look at her. "Mayhap," he agreed. "And who would wish to make the President look thusly?"

They answered together : "Mr. Jefferson."

"I think," Elizabeth finished in an even quieter whisper, "that Mr. Jefferson wanted to have someone he could trust among Mr. Marshall's party to France, someone who could observe, and be privy to everything, all the goings on, and who could report back," she theorized.

Maybe Sam would think such convoluted fancies and taste for subterfuge a result of her recent acquaintance with Lewis' 'The Monk.' But she had her suspicions, nonetheless.

Her husband just nodded at her. "Aye. That way, Mr. Jefferson would know of anything that could damage the President's reputation and be able to turn it to his advantage," Sam agreed. "You may be right, wife," he said then in a normal voice. "And never let me think for a moment that your mind is not as sharp or analytical as anyone's," he added with a chuckle and a fond look.

# CHAPTER TWENTY TWO

"So what was the talk at the tavern?" Izzy asked boldly after dinner was over and they had adjourned to the River Room. Elizabeth had said she would play for them, and was busily sorting through her music to find pretty, lively songs she liked and a few she thought she might ask Izzy to sing, as well. Izzy's voice was especially suited to the lilting airs Elizabeth favored, and the timbres of their two voices when they sang together blended well, so a couple of duets made it onto the music rack.

"Oh, they all wanted to hear the latest from Charlottesville," Josh said lightly, but a long look passed between him and his wife.

They had discussed just how much to tell Sam and Elizabeth about what Josh had really been doing in France and among the Marshall envoys, and had decided to stick to generalities. This was more for their in-laws' sake than their own.

However, Izzy had been getting the feeling that Elizabeth, at least, suspected that there was more to it than they had said. She wondered if Sam suspected, too.

Now, Sam replied that they'd heard that a piece of property across the river might be for sale soon, and Sam was excited at the prospect of expanding the farm. He had a sturdy, reliable team of workers who cared for the vast acreage he had already acquired, and told his wife and Izzy that he felt sure he could hire additional men to work the new acreage. Since his interest was now really in the sawmills he had established, such delegation was a necessity.

"This property—is it anywhere near that area you spoke of before, where you think a ferry might be possible?" Izzy asked innocently.

Sam gave her a sharp look. "Aye, sister, 'tis."

"So you would benefit by having the ferry terminals on your property, too, of course," Izzy noted with an answering grin.

"Aye, there is that, too," Sam agreed. "I wonder if our young brother Jesse might not be a good man for the job, if it can be accomplished, and if we can seek Mr. Little's assistance in fashioning a ferry boat," he added, mentioning a local carpenter and cabinet maker.

"Does he make boats?" Izzy asked, curious. She knew that carpenters also doubled as undertakers, since they made coffins, but ferry boats?

"'Tis likely we shall have to inquire of other ferrymen and ask where they had their conveyances built," Sam admitted. "But 'twill be no trouble to do that," he finished with certainty.

Josh just shook his head in admiration. He didn't know anyone who could envision, plan ahead and take advantage of opportunities the way his brother could.

"And then there was news out of Tunkhannock that a prisoner has escaped," Josh put in next.

"A prisoner?" Elizabeth queried from behind the pianoforte. She looked up, alarmed, from the stacks of sheet music she was going through.

"Aye," Sam replied gravely. "They think as he most likely will have gone down river, towards the valley," he reassured everyone. "But 'tis no way to be certain," he added.

"What was he in jail for?" Izzy asked, curious.

"Thievery," Sam replied shortly. "The man had stolen two horses."

"Ah, then, he very likely stole a third to make his escape!" Izzy rejoined merrily. "Any reports of stolen mounts in the Tunkhannock area?"

Sam and Josh shook their heads, as they did not know. "But the sheriff and his men are searching for him," Sam added.

Elizabeth began to play, then, and Sam lit his pipe, and Josh and Izzy sat back on the cushioned settee, hand in hand, and just listened happily.

Many of the pieces Elizabeth played were dance tunes, and would likely be heard on the thirty-first, at the Christmas Ball. Since it was the evening, now, of the twenty-eighth, the next day, Saturday, would be the last visiting day of the old year. Sunday was for church and family, and then Monday would be the Ball, with the day being spent getting ready. After New Year's Day, there would be more visiting, and the back and forth of carriages and traps would be heard until the Twelfth Night celebration on January 6.

"I am sure you have heard most of these before," Elizabeth said after she had played 'Les Plaisirs de Flore,' 'Lady Nelson's Waltz,' and something called 'Buonaparte's Expedition.'

Izzy said that yes, she was familiar with most of the tunes so far, as she and Josh had attended numerous balls in Charlottesville and elsewhere since their marriage. "Play some more—if you're not tired," she asked.

Elizabeth said she felt quite well and played 'Love in a Village,' 'Sweet Richard,' and several more tunes that had her small audience tapping their toes.

Next, Elizabeth called Izzy up to sing, and together they performed 'Oh Nanny Wilt Thou Gang With Me,' 'Robin Adair,' 'The Linnet' and 'Auld Lang Syne.' Josh and Sam joined in on the last, and they decided that since the next day was once again very busy, they should call it a night.

The next afternoon, Izzy and Elizabeth set out, once again in the carriage, for their calls. Elizabeth wore her brand new rose colored damask gown that Martha had whipped up according to her and Izzy's preferences. It was much admired as they went among yet more of their acquaintances in Laceyville, Skinner's Eddy and Black Walnut.

Although men did not 'visit' *per se,* they did call on friends and family, especially at this time of year. Sam spent a couple of hours at his mills in the morning, and then he and Josh rode out to spend a little time with an elderly acquaintance who lived in Auburn.

Hugo Vanderlip's family had owned much of the land now owned by Ebenezer Skinner in the area east of Braintrim Village. His older brother Frederick had had a farm very near where the Reverend Sturdevant built his own home, and while the three families were not related by blood, they had always been close associates both in business and socially.

Hugo was the youngest sibling and the last one still living when the new century dawned. In his late 70's, he was considered quite elderly at the time, and was largely house-bound as he suffered chronic debilitation and pain from injuries he sustained in the French and Indian War and in the Revolution, where he had fought on the side of the Colonists.

The Auburn church and community generally took care of 'Uncle Hugo' as he'd come to be known, making sure he had food, enough wood for the fireplace, and other necessities. Although Hugo was still able to care for himself, and although his mind was very sharp, his world had become smaller as his mobility had declined. While most of the time he was quite content to watch the birds and other wildlife that he could see from his window, and read, and think, visits from people outside his community were always welcome, for they usually brought news of the wider world.

Josh's visit with his brother Sam was a double joy for the old man, because not only did Hugo consider Sam quite the visionary and businessman, Josh now lived in Virginia, and could bring news of the great men running the country.

After offering tea, which Josh and Sam accepted but Sam made, encouraging his host to sit and rest while he took care of things, Hugo listened avidly to Josh's re-telling of his trip to France, and of the politics going on currently in the Capital. Hugo was also eager to know if Washington, D.C. would be occupied shortly by Congress and the President.

"I do not think it will be ready this spring," Josh replied with a shake of his head. "Perhaps, though, around the time of the election."

Sam brought over mugs of tea at this juncture, and a tin of biscuits he'd found in the cupboard.

"Those be nice ones, they be," Hugo said of the biscuits, taking two. "Mrs. Keppell from the church made 'em and I don't mind telling you that when they have gone I hope she finds it in her heart, and her larder, to make some more!" the old man declared. "So, Mr. Sturdevant, who do you think will be the next President?" he asked brightly, turning to Josh.

"I know Mr. Jefferson intends to stand for the office, against President Adams."

"Aye, the President would like a second term," put in Sam.

"Oh, yes, yes, of course, who would not?" Hugo chimed in testily. "But this XYZ business, well, you yourself must have seen it, Mr. Sturdevant, having been in the thick of it over there in France?" he prodded.

Josh just gave him a nod.

"The way the President handled the information about the mission did not gain him favor," commented Sam as he took a sip of tea.

Everyone agreed about that, and Josh steered the conversation more towards the coming election than the previous year's mission to France.

"Mr. Jefferson is convinced that we must fund a standing Army and Navy, and gives the troubles we have had with France as a case in point of our need for both," Josh told Hugo.

"But another tax!" decried Hugo, and clicked his tongue and wagged his head.

"'Tis true that a tax is the proposed funding source," Sam agreed. "But how else could the country be certain of ongoing support?" he queried reasonably.

"And 'twould not be so much for each person that it would be a hardship," Josh continued.

"Then would it be enough to build an Army and expand our Navy?" Hugo asked pointedly.

Josh nodded. "Mr. Jefferson says so. You see, a little bit, given by many, can be quite a lot."

Hugo made a noise that sounded as though he wasn't yet convinced of the truth of that statement, but said no more.

"Mr. Jefferson is also in favor of repealing the Alien and Sedition Acts," Josh said then.

"Ah, yes! Now those: President Adams and the Federalists would have us believe they strengthen national security," Hugo replied cannily.

Josh smiled: Hugo's mind was sharper than those of many men half his age. "Aye," he replied.

"But Mr. Jefferson feels the Acts are mere vehicles to keep those who do not agree with the Federalist Party's views from expressing their own," Josh explained.

"For example, look at the way the Acts have been invoked to get rid of some newspaper editors, or at least have them pull various stories and opinion pieces from publication," Sam offered.

Josh reminded them of Bill Durrell, the first editor arrested under the Acts, for reprinting part of an article that was critical of the President. "The threat of a trial has made Mr. Durrell shut down his paper and he is now a pauper," Josh told them sadly. "He most fears imprisonment, for he has a large family to support—somehow."

"And he cannot do that from a jail cell," put in Sam.

"Of course, the Acts were crafted and aimed against Benjamin Bache," Josh confirmed.

"His *Advertiser* out of Philadelphia was a publication I read as often as I could lay my hands on a copy!" Sam declared.

"Yes, 'twas a good paper," Hugo agreed.

Josh lowered his voice. "D'you realize that Bache and his wife were threatened?" he asked. "Their home was vandalized as well, by some of

Adams' cronies," Josh added. "And he was physically attacked, more than once, before he died."

Bache had died of yellow fever during the epidemic in 1798.

"And James Bell, down in Carlisle, I heard he was arrested for printing what they called treason in his *Independent*," Sam said. "Though I know not what the outcome was."

"I always liked what the *Boston Chronicle* had to say, myself," Hugo put in, then.

"How did you obtain that?" Sam asked, curious. Boston was quite far away, even though it was emotionally, perhaps, close, because most of the area's residents had come to Pennsylvania from New England originally.

Hugo explained that his niece lived near Boston and had periodically sent a *Chronicle* to him while it was still operational. The newspaper had been sold a few months before, and oddly enough the editor had died a week after that. "They are usually a month or so out of date, but the news was still good," Hugo said cheerily.

Josh enumerated the dreadful things some Massachusetts Federalists had done to the editor of the *Chronicle*. Ironically, his surname had been Adams, like that of the President against whom he so freely spoke. For his outspoken opinions, the editor had been drummed out of the Fire Company to which he'd belonged, called an anarchist, and charged with several counts of libel. "Mr. Jefferson told me that on his death bed, Editor Adams said he regretted nothing, and remained attached to the liberties of our country which, in his opinion, the Federalists were hostile towards," Josh finished solemnly. "'Tis widely thought the tribulations he suffered at the hands of the Federalists were what deteriorated his health."

"'Tis not right," Hugo said firmly. "Our Constitution guarantees us the right to free speech, and newspapers are a part of that: they must not be gagged in any way and their publishers should no more be attacked and vilified than any other citizen!"

"Ah, but there are many who have suffered because of the Acts," Josh went on. "A score, at least. And it is all part of the Federalists' major tenet of centralization," Josh said. "They feel everything should be run out of the Federal government, with virtually no states' rights."

"Whereas Mr. Jefferson espouses not only states' rights but local governmental rights," Sam noted. "You see how important the town meetings are in this region," he added with a nod.

They spoke then of the way the town meetings had informed residents about the expansion currently being enjoyed in Braintrim Village, the Eddy, and Black Walnut.

"An involved and informed citizenry is a nation's greatest asset," Sam opined.

The afternoon passed very quickly, and it was nearing dusk when Sam and Josh turned their horses towards home. 'Uncle Hugo' had been delighted with the visit, and would reminisce about the lively discussion for many weeks to come.

# CHAPTER TWENTY THREE

The next day, Sunday, Izzy convinced Josh to go with her to see if the Susquehanna River was as frozen over as it appeared. They had all gone to church in the morning, then come home to dinner, but the afternoon was open.

Although the clear water of the river could be seen right along the shore in the spots where the water was very shallow and the sun had melted the top ice, Izzy was able to step out about a foot onto solid ice, then quickly walk a couple more feet towards the middle of the river.

"The ice feels pretty solid here, Josh," she called to her husband, her breath making little white plumes as she spoke. "Come on, join me: let's see how far we can go!" she teased.

Josh shook his head. As a precaution, he'd brought a length of stout rope, which he'd tied around a nearby tree trunk: 'just in case,' he'd said. He had also told Sam and Elizabeth where they were going and Sam had promised to check on them through a window from time to time.

''Tis a foolish notion, do you not think?' Sam had asked Josh.

'Aye. But Izzy is rarely foolish,' Josh had replied. 'I think she just wants an adventure.'

In fact, Josh assumed that Izzy somehow knew, or had read, of the river having frozen over during this winter, and so thought walking on it would be safe. He never asked her, though. And he could hardly try to explain his reasoning to Sam!

'I see—it must be rather dull here for her, then,' Sam had remarked, sounding resigned.

'No, no, 'tis not that at all,' Josh had replied quickly, adding that both he and Izzy were greatly enjoying their visit, and didn't find life in Braintrim a bit 'dull!' 'In truth, brother, we both are sad to see the end of our time here approaching so quickly,' Josh had added.

Their visit, which had seemed an endless stretch of days upon their arrival the week before, was now nearly half gone, and the upcoming days, Josh knew, would go very fast.

Now, from the shore, he answered his wife, "no, Izzy, what if you fall in? Who will rescue you if I'm out there on the ice with you, or worse still, if I fall in too?" he asked reasonably.

Giggling, Izzy shook her head. "'Tis very firm," she said of the ice. "Look, I'm being cautious: I try each step to see if I hear any cracking..." she protested, defending herself as she made a few more hesitant steps out towards the small island that was several yards off the northern bank of the river.

The current slowed in this portion of the Susquehanna. As it was a bend, that was natural on the north side, but the island between the two banks also produced a further retardation in the flow of water on the northern side. Things were different on the southern side, but where Izzy was, the water flowed more languidly and thus froze a bit more readily.

Josh watched as Izzy slowly traversed the entire stretch of ice between the shore and the island. Moments later, she gained the snowy bank of the deserted hump of land, and crowed with delight.

"I made it!" she called out, and waved. Then she turned, and headed off into the underbrush and the small stand of hemlocks that stood on the island. Her green cloak melted into the trees, and Josh felt his belly tighten with fear.

"Izzy! Izzy! At least stay where I can see you!" he called, cupping his hands around his mouth to make his entreaty travel farther.

Behind him, Sam and Elizabeth, both wrapped in warm cloaks, came to stand on the river's edge and watch for their sister in law.

"We heard you shouting: where is she?" Elizabeth asked.

"She went for a walk," Josh replied, his tone both censorious and disbelieving.

"Where?" Sam asked, confounded.

"On the island."

Sam and Elizabeth both looked at the island in question.

"I do not see her," Sam said gravely.

"Nor I."

"Well, I don't suppose she can get into much mischief on an island the size of your kitchen garden, Elizabeth," Josh said, but he didn't feel as confident as his words. Always, in the back of his mind, was the possibility that Izzy might stumble upon another one of those 'time vortices' like the one she had stepped through initially. And then, she might disappear. And then, she might never return.

"I doubt if there are any animals on the island that could do her harm," mused Sam.

A pair of large birds which had been camouflaged by the tops of the trees suddenly exploded into flight, circling the small island and peering down at it.

"They look upset," commented Sam.

Seconds later, Izzy dashed out of the trees and made for the shore and the iced over river. She retraced her steps in a fraction of the time it had taken her to cross over, and within a couple of minutes she was grabbing Josh's hand and gaining the shore below the Sturdevant home.

"Bald eagles," she breathed, grinning widely. The bird had been the new nation's symbol for almost two decades, and to Izzy they were a rare sighting because many fewer existed in her own time. In 1800, however, the birds were quite plentiful. "A nest of them, up in the trees!" she declared. "I didn't mean to disturb them, but…"

"But they are not used to having human beings come crashing up onto their island," Josh finished for her, sounding both relieved and severe.

"Well, I didn't hurt them!" Izzy declared stoutly. "I didn't even see the babies, though I heard them squawking, funny little things…"

"You must be frozen: come inside and have some tea," Elizabeth urged.

"I'm not cold, not one bit of it!" Izzy declared, still grinning. "Let's all go ice skating!"

There was no talking her out of it, and since Sam and Josh did have fond memories of skating at Spring Hill Pond, they bundled the children along with Becky, Belinda, Ephraim and Roger, and set off in the large carriage to go to the well known skating pond. Martha happily stayed home with Cordelia, after fussing to make sure everyone was dressed warmly enough.

The adults rented skates, and the little ones just held onto their parents' hands and slid along, their eyes wide and their mouths opened in nearly constant screams of excitement and joy.

Elizabeth proved to be the best among them, steady and slow, she held onto Sam's arm most of the time, but when he lost his balance and slipped to the ice's surface, Elizabeth stayed standing, her two sons holding on—Peter to one hand and John to the side of his mother's skirts.

Josh only fell once, but Izzy fell a couple of times, laughing as she did and still laughing when she got up and brushed herself off.

"I never was very good at skating," she giggled.

"You have ice skated before?" Elizabeth asked. "I did not realize it got cold enough in France for ponds to freeze over?"

Oops: she'd done it again, Izzy realized quickly. "Well, not normal ponds, but, erm, the Queen had a little skating pond at the Hameau," she extemporized. "It is no more than two feet deep, so it freezes even if the surrounding natural ponds do not. I have skated there."

Elizabeth looked suitably impressed at the thought of Izzy ice skating with the late Queen, and said nothing more.

Monday morning, Izzy admitted to Josh that she ached in several places due to her exertions the day before, and her falls at the pond.

"But it was worth it: what a fun day!" she claimed, even as she winced trying to reach behind her to pull her stays tight. She gave up, and reached over for the quilted 'jumps' that would be perfectly appropriate for a day at home: as they were only lightly boned, they were far more comfortable.

Most of the rest of the day was spent in preparation for the ball that evening. Suits and waist coats were laid out and discussed and finally chosen. Gowns the same, and once chosen, fans, reticules and shawls to coordinate were offered, rejected, and finally accepted.

Dinner mid day was eaten in an atmosphere of anticipation and afterwards, Elizabeth settled the boys down for their naps while Izzy nursed Cordelia.

"She is such a good child," Elizabeth said, low, entering her sitting area on the top floor of the house. Izzy was in a wide old rocking chair with her baby, who was falling asleep as she finished nursing.

"She is," Izzy agreed, gently unlatching the baby and moving her to her shoulder to burp her. A few minutes later, the little girl was fast asleep in her cradle.

Water was brought up from the river, and strained and then boiled, and the big copper tub in the Keeping Room was readied for everyone's baths.

Izzy recalled that on her first visit she had been the first to bathe, and had not realized the honor such a move truly was until she saw Elizabeth and then the rest of the family bathe after her, using pretty much the same water.

This day, Martha had built up the fire until it roared in the huge square stone chimney and put the temperature of the Keeping Room at a nice, toasty level. The big copper tub was lined with fresh lengths of linen to keep bathers from burning themselves against the hot copper sides of the bath. Then boiling water was poured in to a depth of about a foot, and mixed with fresh cold water until the temperature was bearable.

Izzy was once again the first to be invited to bathe, and she luxuriated in the hot soapy water, taking care to wash and rinse her hair thoroughly, and being careful of the tender spots forming as a result of her falls the day before. Luckily, none of the bruises was visible, since she'd fallen on her hips and rear. She thought, however, that she might just avail herself of some willow bark tea before they left for the ball, to take the edge off the aches. At least, until the punch at the ball kicked in!

Elizabeth followed Izzy in the big tub, and then Josh and Sam, and then with everyone clean and fresh, it was time to dress for the ball.

"My stays are too tight, loosen them a bit, Belinda," Izzy begged. It was nearing time to leave for the ball, and she was in Elizabeth and Sam's bedchamber, where the two women were, with Belinda as lady's maid, getting ready.

"I cannot let them out too much, Ma'am, or the gown will not fall right," Belinda replied in her gentle voice. Still, she worked one slender finger beneath the bottom most lacings and let them out a scant amount.

Izzy sighed. "Better."

Elizabeth gave her sister in law an appraising look. "That is a beautiful gown, Izzy. But will you not trip on the train?" she queried.

Izzy's gown was the color of old gold, accented with a black velvet band at its Empire waistline, and on its sleeves. Behind, a bow at the waist in that same velvet cascaded down atop the watered silk and pooled in a small train of about two feet in length. Tiny gold bells on the sleeves chimed softly whenever she moved.

"Aha, lookie here," Izzy crowed, and lifted the hem of the gown to show a small button sewn into the inside hem and a loop just above the bottom of the him, also on the inside. "See? I just fasten it so, *et voilà*! No train. And the front of the hem does not brush the floor, so I should be all right," she added, unbuttoning the hem and letting the train fall.

"Why, how clever!" Elizabeth declared. "It makes the gown much more useful," she agreed.

"Yes, and I don't mind telling you that with what I paid for this gown, I want to be able to wear it as often as possible!" Izzy declared with a laugh.

Izzy had fixed a slender band of gold accented with small diamonds in her hair that Belinda had twisted and braided into a rather elaborate creation. Diamond drop earrings and a gold and diamond pendant necklace with delicate filigree completed her outfit along with a black fan and the *de rigueur* above-the -elbow white gloves.

"Well, 'tis lovely," Elizabeth sighed.

"So is yours," Izzy declared. "And the color is perfect for you," she added.

Elizabeth's gown was a rather stunning silk brocade in pale blue and silver, its high waist accented with silver braid as were the edges of the delicate cap sleeves. The gown had no train, but Elizabeth carried a silver gilt silk fan and Belinda had woven a silver ribbon through her upswept blonde curls.

"One more thing…" Izzy murmured, and pawed through the little satchel of accessories she had brought with her, and had taken to Elizabeth's bed chamber, just in case they needed anything. "Here…" She lifted out a fluffy white plume, and stepped over to Elizabeth, eyeing her head critically. "There we are," she said, inserting the quill end of the feather amidst Elizabeth's curls and fixing it with a hair pin.

Elizabeth peered at her reflection in the little mirror that was perched on her dressing table. "It does look fine…but do you think it is a bit too fancy?" she asked uncertainly.

"Not a bit of it," Izzy answered stoutly. In fact, it looked fabulous. But she knew Elizabeth was unused to wearing such fashionable accessories: the ribbon had been daring enough for her! Izzy had actually been relieved that her sister in law hadn't chosen to wear a cap with her ball gown: such things were done, of course, but usually by much older matrons.

"Shall I ask Sam what he thinks?" Elizabeth queried, still unsure. She was delighted by what she saw in the mirror, but not positive it wasn't too frivolous a style for the daughter in law of Braintrim Village's leading minister.

Izzy started to say that her brother in law wouldn't know a plume from a drab from a horse tail, but bit her lip, and went to fetch Sam, who was dressing with his twin, in the second bedchamber.

When Sam, followed closely by Josh, arrived seconds later, he pronounced his wife 'ravishingly lovely,' and kissed her soundly on her cheek; everyone smiled happily.

Both Sturdevant men wore dark frock coats, elaborately embroidered waist coats—gold for Josh and silver for Sam— snowy white shirts and cravats, yellow knee breeches and silk hose with black buckled shoes. The Christmas Ball was probably the most formal event of the year in Braintrim and surrounding towns, and everyone wanted to look their best.

## CHAPTER TWENTY FOUR

It was with a sense of *déjà-vû* that Izzy climbed into the carriage that evening. They sat exactly as they had before: the ladies on one side, the men on the other, as their horses carried them gently over the packed dirt roadway that would become Old Route 6 and eventually Main Street, Laceyville in Izzy's time.

What would her life have been, she wondered, (not for the first time) had she not gone to that dance back in 1795? What if she had never fallen in love with Josh? What if he hadn't fallen in love with her?

She had taken the liberty of researching him when she'd returned to her own time. She had discovered that, despite the promise and potential she had observed in Joshua Sturdevant when she had met him, modern day resources spoke only of an unremarkable life—barely a footnote to the far more illustrious accounts of his twin brother Sam's life.

It had been that unhappy discovery as well as her own feelings for the man which had prompted her to set her modern life in order and return to 1795. Now, it had been four years to the day since she had found herself standing at the Sturdevant home's wide-planked front door in a snowstorm, knocking, and seeing Josh's beloved but startled face as he had opened it.

She looked across the carriage at her husband. What an amazing four years it had been! And was she happy? Oh, indeed. And Josh's career looked to become all she, and he, had hoped it might be. Firmly among Jefferson's most intimate coterie, both of them were poised, Izzy thought, to become one of the first families of Charlottesville—and possibly Washington, once Jefferson won the Presidency.

They had a beautiful family, a lovely home, and even though she occasionally had a niggling bit of guilt about having returned and changed Josh's original destiny, she usually was able to shake that off and convince herself that his more prominent life would not affect the future in any material way.

And even though she once in a while slipped and said something peculiar, she by and large had kept her great secret—that she was from the twenty-first century, not the eighteenth—something only she and Josh knew. And of course, Mr. Jefferson knew, as well: Izzy had made a real blunder when he'd been a guest at their June, 1796 wedding, and circumstances had forced her to tell him where she was from. To his credit, the man had believed her completely, and also to his credit, he had never inquired of her what his own future might hold.

However, Izzy was under no illusions that her 'future knowledge' might not be a big motivating factor in Mr. Jefferson's inclusion of her—the only woman—in his 'inner circle.'

As the carriage trundled along now, she remembered the evening more than two years before when, after a quiet dinner at Monticello with Jefferson and a few other friends, the three of them had been left alone as the remaining guests had taken their leave.

Jefferson had then explained to Josh what he hoped he could accomplish in France. They had all still been in the dining room at Monticello, lingering over some excellent brandy, and Jefferson had doused all but the large candelabrum in the center of his dining room table.

Izzy had sat to his right, and Josh to his left, and Jefferson, at the head of the table, had faced the windows that gave out onto the dark gardens. Overhead, the skylight had shown only stars, for the moon had set. It had been June, 1797, and warm, so there had been no fire.

Jefferson had had no need to tell Josh and Izzy of his dislike of the President or his disdain for the Federalist Party in general: both were at opposition, at almost every turn, to his own opinions. But he had begun nonetheless with a feelingly put summary of his grievances.

Then, he had spoken of the upset caused to the French by the Jay Treaty, and summarized the most recent attacks on the U.S. merchant ships.

'Something must be done,' Jefferson had said in a low voice. He had sent all his servants to bed, but one never knew who might be lingering on the other side of the revolving serving door, or listening up through the dumb waiter. 'The French, as you well know, will not come to us, *bicorne*, as it were, in hand, and ask for a similar agreement. The President intends to send a delegation over, to speak with the Ambassador, Talleyrand.'

Josh had looked surprised. 'Who is in the delegation?' he had asked in a whisper.

Jefferson had replied that the French Ambassador that Washington had appointed, Charles Pinckney, was one of them. Elbridge Gerry, a statesman whose views were very much in line with Jefferson's, was the second. And John Marshall, a Congressman from Virginia who was a staunch Federalist, was the third.

'I can see why President Adams would send Pinckney and Marshall, but Gerry?' Josh had asked.

Jefferson had shrugged. 'Should negotiations not proceed as planned, I have no doubt that Mr. Gerry is there to take the blame,' he had opined wryly.

He had paused, and Izzy and Josh had looked at him expectantly.

'I believe this entire matter to be one of great— fragility,' he had said, then. 'If not handled correctly, our relationship with France might be detrimentally affected for decades to come. And in any event, if it is handled poorly, the entire escapade might reflect so badly on Mr. Adams, that winning the Presidency in 1800 will be made a much easier task for me,' Jefferson had confided.

'Indeed, it would,' Josh had agreed. 'But you cannot ensure such a result…can you?' he had asked, knowing the answer.

Jefferson had given his protégé a tired smile. 'If I knew what was going on, step by step, as the delegation proceeded to meet with Talleyrand and speak to him, then perhaps I could, if not ensure, then at least influence, the result,' he had murmured. 'I want you, Josh, to go with Mr. Marshall to France, as his Chief Aide,' Jefferson had announced then.

Josh had looked taken aback, but Izzy had smiled.

'Your fluency in French, thanks to your remarkable wife who has so ably instructed you,' Jefferson continued, with a fond look over at Izzy, 'makes you an ideal candidate. Not to mention your experience in legal and governmental matters.'

'But—my politics, sir: I am no more in President Adams' camp than Mr. Gerry!' Josh had protested.

To his credit, he did not mention the fact that his first born, Nicholas, was but four months old at the time, and that he might be needed at home. He knew Izzy was completely able to cope.

'Aye, and that is the thing of it, Josh,' Jefferson had enthused. 'You are my creature, my eyes and ears, as it were, my wolf in sheep's clothing amidst the flock!'

The Vice President had continued then to explain that he had already spoken to Marshall about Josh, making it sound as though he regretted it mightily that the young lawyer was so necessary to him stateside that he could not even consider the possibility of loaning him to Marshall for the mission to France. 'I told him I was aggrieved at the impossibility, because your demeanor, your experience and your gift of fluency in the French language would have made you a perfect aide to him in the delegation,' Jefferson had continued on a chuckle.

'So of course,' Izzy had put in with a smile, 'Mr. Marshall decided he just had to have Josh, whether you could spare him or not, and perhaps mostly because you said you could not spare him, am I right, Mr. Vice President?'

Jefferson had urged both her and Josh to call him 'Thomas' since he called them by their first names, even calling Josh by the diminutive of his, though he stuck to 'Isabeau' for Izzy. But somehow, Izzy just couldn't do that, and even Josh usually got around it by calling Jefferson 'sir.'

Jefferson had given Izzy an answering smile and nodded jubilantly. 'Precisely! So Mr. Marshall is very eager that I should somehow persuade you to join his delegation, as his Chief Aide no less,' Jefferson had told Josh then.

'And you wish me to do this, and to—be your eyes and ears, as you say?' Josh had asked. His voice had been even, but Izzy could sense that the idea excited him.

Jefferson had nodded. 'If you will.'

'But—how shall I relay to you what goes on?' Josh had asked then. 'Surely communiqués through the usual channels will be monitored?'

'Aye, 'tis right, of course, but there are ways for you to send word back to me, erm, outside the usual channels,' he had said, and Izzy had envisioned a network of shadowy sailors and horsemen entrusted to carry secret missives to the Vice President.

Her vision had not been far off the mark, for Jefferson knew people on both sides of the Atlantic who could be trusted to perform such tasks—for a price. And it was a price he was able, and happy, to pay.

'And,' the Vice President had continued, 'your notes to me, if discovered by parties which are against us, will look completely benign: no more interesting than a discussion of the weather, or the birds you have seen, and the food you have eaten.'

Josh had frowned, as had Izzy. But then Izzy's brow had cleared and her face had sparked with excitement. 'You've made a code book!' she whispered triumphantly.

Jefferson had withdrawn from his breast pocket a small sheaf of paper on which a number of words had been written. 'I did, indeed.'

It turned out that the code Jefferson had devised was fairly easy to memorize: that way, Josh had not even needed to carry the code book with him, just in case he was suspected. He had been instructed by Jefferson to write daily, if need be, detailing everything that Marshall, Pinckney and Gerry did, everyone with whom they spoke, and any other conversations or events which Josh might think important.

'I trust your judgement on this,' Jefferson had told Josh, and had given him a firm hand shake when Josh had agreed to the mission.

They had departed for their home in Charlottesville, then, and Jefferson had kissed Izzy warmly on the cheek as she had stepped into their carriage.

'If you have need of anything at all whilst your husband is away at my bidding, you have only to contact me, and it shall be done,' he had whispered to her, and Izzy had pressed his hand in thanks.

She had climbed in, then, and watched through the coach window as Jefferson had returned to his gracious home. She'd waved, and he had lifted a hand in return just as the shadowy figure of a woman had glided along the large front windows and moved to stand at his side. She had been back lit by the candelabrum Jefferson had carried from the dining room to the entrance hall, but Izzy had been able to make out dark hair under a white cap as their carriage rolled away. She had had no doubt then, nor had she doubted since, that this woman was the mysterious Sally Hemings.

Now, she sighed. She had never officially met Sally, although after that first glimpse, she had come across her a couple of times in the gardens at Monticello, when she had been visiting Jefferson with the children. She had also passed Sally, she was sure of it, in the halls at Jefferson's mansion. However, Sally had always cast her eyes down and hurried off after a quickly bobbed curtsey, so Izzy had never had a chance to talk to her.

Well, maybe in the future, she could do that: how fascinating would that be!? she thought to herself as she gazed out the window not of her carriage as it pulled away from Monticello, but of the Sturdevant carriage as it made its way over the frosty ground to the Christmas Ball.

Unlike the journey to the Harvest Ball when she had first arrived in the past, this trip was in winter, over icy roads, and so the horse trod carefully. Still, the four Sturdevants arrived in good time at the hall behind Elizabeth's father's tavern, and made their way towards the entrance with great expectation and delight.

## CHAPTER TWENTY FIVE

A gust of warm, perfumed air greeted them when the doors were opened; Izzy and Elizabeth handed their cloaks to a bewigged gentleman who hovered just inside the hall's foyer and had been tasked with hanging everyone's outer garments on the many hooks and pegs provided.

The inner doors to the hall stood open, for although it was very cold outside, inside the air would become stale and hot very quickly, so some fresh air and circulation was needed. Elizabeth's father and mother stood just inside the second doorway, and greeted those attending the Ball, as the *de facto* hosts.

Ebenezer kissed his daughter, remarked how well she looked, and shook hands with everyone else in the party. Izzy thought Ebenezer's eye twinkled at Elizabeth's jaunty feather, but she was in no doubt as to Eunice's reaction: she clocked the feather and silver ribbon, ran an expert eye over her daughter's ensemble, and broke into a wide smile.

"You are a vision!" she exclaimed, and hugged Elizabeth, who blushed. "As are you!" she turned to Izzy, and kissed her on one cheek. "Every bit the Countess," she added *sotto voce*.

Izzy shook her head, but she knew Eunice Skinner had always been a bit in awe of her assumed identity as 'Isabeau de Villehardouin, Comtesse de

Billy,' and counted it good fortune that 'royalty' had married into their family.

The musicians—Izzy kept calling them the 'band' which made Josh chuckle—were, as before, on the dais at one end of the large hall. A long series of tables holding punches, savories and sweets was against one wall. Groupings of chairs filled the corners and on the wall opposite the refreshments, more chairs were scattered for those who needed to rest from dancing, or who wished to engage in a sit-down conversation.

Apparently, the four Sturdevants had arrived just in time, for the musicians were still tuning up and quaffing a last sip of punch before their first 'set', and the Skinners had not yet taken their places at the top of the line. Quickly, they got in position, as did nearly everyone else in the room, for the opening dance of the evening, like the final dance, was as Izzy would say, a 'big deal.'

With the exception of a few very elderly persons whose gout or other disabilities necessitated their use of a cane, and who were now seated, and gazing at the dancers with delight, remembrance and regret, everyone was in the dance line, which stretched from just below the dais almost to the doors of the hall!

Izzy and Elizabeth found spots about half way down the line, and Josh and Sam stood opposite them. First came the march, where couples—beginning with the Skinners—joined hands and processed down the line and then around the outside to resume their original positions. It was a good chance to see and be seen, and to greet friends and neighbors.

Because of the number of people, this would take about a quarter of an hour, and while they waited their turn, couples were encouraged to talk. Talking during the dancing was a Regency custom that Izzy quite liked, now that she'd become used to the idea.

"I think the entire Village is here, with a few people from further afield," Izzy said to Josh as the couples began to walk down the line.

"Indeed, Sam estimated nearly two hundred folk," her husband replied. "And you are the loveliest woman in the room, Izzy," he told her with a proud smile.

When it was their turn to process, Izzy curtsied prettily and Josh bowed, then they joined hands at shoulder height and walked 'down the line,' smiling and nodding at friends and acquaintances as they did so. Back in their spots, they had a chance to chat a bit more before the dance itself, a familiar one called 'Chestnut,' began.

"I see Elvira Goldner is here," Izzy said with a smile. "And Caroline."

"Aye, I saw them. And I am presuming the young man opposite Caroline in the set is her beau?" Josh replied.

Izzy said she supposed it must be. "Do you know him?" she asked, but Josh shook his head. Turning slightly, he murmured the question to his brother Sam, who murmured back.

"His name is Ronald Chamberlain," Josh informed Izzy in the next moment. "His people are from Wyalusing way but he is with the First Regiment, out of Philadelphia," he concluded.

Izzy had noted the young man's blue military coat with red facings, denoting his membership in a Mid-Atlantic region. "That's quite an honor for him, I mean, to be in the First Regiment, isn't it?" Izzy asked. She was quite fuzzy as to the details of militaria, but she knew that once the Treaty of Versailles had been signed, the United States had disbanded its standing army. Indeed, President Adams contended that the country didn't have the funds to keep a large military force at the ready at the present time, and so there were just two Regiments comprising a few hundred soldiers who were on active duty.

However, Jefferson had often expressed dissatisfaction with this situation, and had revealed to Izzy and Josh his plan to build a Military Academy where future soldiers would receive not only a fine education, but proper training in all aspects of the military. This, he felt, would provide well trained and prepared soldiers for any future needs of the United States.

During this discussion after a quiet dinner with just the three of them at Monticello, Izzy had made one of her 'future knowledge' blunders when, to Jefferson's statement about building an Academy, she'd blurted out, 'oh! West Point!' which had made Jefferson and her husband look at her in confusion.

'You refer to the Army Post, above the Hudson River?' Jefferson had asked. The government had purchased more than a thousand acres a few years before with a mind to expand the Post and perhaps provide a training ground. But there was no formal Academy. Not yet.

'Erm...uhm...yes, I, uh, I thought that since that post is the longest continually operating one in the country, it might be a good place to locate the Academy," Izzy had replied, thinking quickly and hoping what she remembered from her history class was correct.

'Indeed, 'tis,' Jefferson had commented thoughtfully.  He had thought much the same thing. Although Jefferson had not referred to the Academy again, Izzy knew that in two short years the U.S. Military Academy would be formally established, one of Jefferson's first major acts as President, and one of his most enduring.

At present, the Regiments were mostly engaged in driving Native Americans off their land and onto 'reservations.' But Jefferson correctly felt that before long, the new United States would need to defend itself, or be drawn into other conflicts, and would have need of an army to fight alongside its new Navy; the Navy had been established during the Revolution.

Now, Josh nodded in agreement. "Aye, 'tis. But he is of good family, and is already a First Lieutenant," he told Izzy.

The dance itself began at this point, everyone having finished processing, or marching, the line. The dancers broke into groups of eight, and began the figures—mostly walking and weaving around one another in various patterns—with those in their group. Eunice Skinner, as 'first lady' of the dance, called the figures, even though almost everyone dancing knew the steps and their sequence inside and out.

After this, the musicians struck up a livelier dance called an 'Allemande,' and after that, Izzy said she needed some punch.

## CHAPTER TWENTY SIX

"They have captured the escapee," announced Mrs. Isaac Lacey, who along with her oldest daughter Mary, called Polly, was supervising the refreshments tables.

"Have they?!" Izzy replied happily, and accepted a cup of punch from the woman. "How wonderful! Do you know any details?" she asked.

Lydia Pratt Lacey fixed Izzy with a stern look. "They likely be unseemly details for a Ball, Mrs. Sturdevant, but I daresay the sheriff might know," she murmured with a nod to that official, who stood near the doors to the hall. An elderly woman whom Izzy thought was the sheriff's mother, sat hunched in a chair next to him. But her toe tapped to the music, which had progressed into a reel.

"Ah, well, perhaps my husband can inquire of him," Izzy said by way of apology for her forthrightness. But inside, she was chuckling.

"Oh, Mother, here is Caroline!" Mary 'Polly' said a moment later. "May I have leave to visit with her?" she entreated.

Mrs. Lacey gave her daughter permission, and the young woman, dressed in a cherry red gown of fine wool, slipped from behind the table to join her friend. Izzy observed Elvira Goldner introducing

Mary Lacey to Lt. Chamberlain and the latter clicking his heels and bowing. Nice manners, she thought.

"'Tis her first dance, she is but fifteen," Mrs. Lacey then told Izzy in a loud whisper.

"Ah, and I'm sure she's enjoying it. Her gown is lovely."

Mrs. Lacey beamed. "Mr. Lacey wove that cloth himself, he did, with a mind that it would be made up into her first ball gown," she said with pride.

"It's beautiful," Izzy commented, just as Elvira Goldner approached. "Hello, Mrs. Goldner," she said with a smile.

That lady returned her smile, then was served a glass of punch by Mrs. Lacey. Izzy was happy to see that there was no enmity between the two women, and that Mrs. Lacey did not ignore Elvira as Mrs. Nabb had.

Fortunately, perhaps, Mrs. Nabb was not in attendance at the ball.

"If it please you, Mrs. Lacey, I should like to visit with you Tuesday next," said Elvira then. "Will you be at home?"

Lydia Lacey nodded. "Aye, though 'tis not my 'at home' day," she replied cautiously.

Elvira smiled. "And might Mr. Lacey also be available?" she asked. "I have a matter to discuss with you both."

Looking pleasantly intrigued, Mrs. Lacey agreed that surely her husband would be happy to come speak with Mrs. Goldner. As it was, the Lacey Draper's Shop in the Village stocked yarn from the Goldners' sheep; Izzy suspected that Elvira was planning to show the Laceys their new multi-toned yarn and the kind of goods it could be used to make, with an eye to them carrying the yarn, and possibly some shawls. She was pleased that the woman had taken her suggestions for marketing the beautiful shawls.

They chatted companionably, and then Izzy said she wanted to find a chair for a bit: she wasn't tired, but she expected to dance a lot throughout the evening, and wanted to pace herself.

Elvira, conveniently, was asked to join in the next dance, and so Izzy slipped into a small straight backed chair. Very shortly, she was joined by Mrs. Bunnell and Mrs. Farley, both residents of the Village and mother and daughter, whom Izzy knew from Church.

Both ladies were on the Sturdevants' visiting list for the following week, but both were happy to find Izzy on her own and available for a chat: she was the exotic foreigner who now lived near the nation's new capital!

"Why, Mrs. Farley, you look a bit pale," Izzy said as she regarded her companion. Maybe it was the dark green of her gown, but the woman looked peaked.

Mrs. Farley, a woman about Izzy's age, shook her lace-capped brown curls ever so slightly and gave a small smile. "No, I am quite well, Mrs. Sturdevant," she replied reassuringly. Then she leaned over and whispered, "but this shall be the last Ball I attend for a time," she said quietly. "Indeed, I am happy for the current fashion, for it enables one to disguise one's condition far longer than previous styles," she added with a chuckle.

"It was that long opening march and dance," judged Mrs. Bunnell, sounding stern and motherly. "It was too long on your feet. You must rest, now, and have some punch."

"Yes, mother," Mrs. Farley responded meekly.

Mrs. Bunnell stepped away to get the punch while Izzy turned to Beth Farley.

"Well, congratulations!" Izzy said. "How many children will this make?" she asked.

"Five," Beth replied with a smile. "We hope for another son, but it feels like a girl," she added with a wry expression. "And you and Mr. Sturdevant have children?" she asked, although she knew very well that they did.

Izzy replied that they had a son, Nicholas, and a daughter, Cordelia. "And I hope we have more children, as well, for I should like a big family," Izzy said.

Now that she was sitting down, Izzy finally had a real chance to admire the decorations in the hall. She remembered that the Harvest Dance had featured corn stalks and similar seasonal items. This Christmas Ball boasted long ropes of white pine looped and swagged and garlanded along the walls and windows and columns of the hall, and tall candles that stood in multi branched candelabra to illuminate the space. Surfaces, like the refreshments table, were swathed in red cloths that contrasted nicely with the white walls, and large pots of red-berried holly stood near the dais.

"Was your journey very arduous?" asked Mrs. Bunnell of Izzy, once she had returned with her daughter's punch.

"Not really, just quite long," Izzy replied.

"And how long do you stay?" Mrs. Bunnell pursued, sipping at her own glass of punch.

Izzy replied that they would leave immediately after Twelfth Night to return to Charlottesville.

"With good weather, we should be back home by the end of the month," she said.

"And your husband, his business is doing well?" Mrs. Bunnell asked, obviously very curious about Josh and Izzy and their life in Virginia.

Izzy replied that her husband's legal practice was thriving, and that he did a good amount of work for Mr. Jefferson, as well.

At this point, feeling quite refreshed, Izzy was happy to see Nathaniel Goldner approaching her, requesting that she partner him in the next dance.

She made her excuses to her companions, and stepped onto the dance floor with the young man.

## CHAPTER TWENTY SEVEN

"What a wonderful night," Izzy breathed. They were in their carriage once more, the horses clop-clopping their careful way west, back towards the Sturdevant home. The dance had ended about a half hour before, and everyone had made their farewells and then turned for home.

"Aye, 'twas that," agreed Sam with a fond look at Izzy, Josh and Elizabeth.

"What time is it?" Izzy asked then, suddenly.

Josh, sitting next to her, and Sam, seated opposite, both pulled out their pocket watches simultaneously and read the dials by the light of the single candle that brightened the interior of the coach.

"I make it midnight," Josh replied with a questioning look at his twin.

Sam nodded.

"Happy New Century," Izzy announced happily.

"Happy New Century!" they echoed.

"I think it will be an amazing one," Izzy predicted mischievously.

"Oh yes?" Elizabeth replied eagerly, snuggling closer to her husband on the carriage seat. "Tell us: why? What do you think will happen? How will 1899 be different from 1799?" she asked in an excited tone.

"Well, as different as 1799 is from 1699!" Izzy replied on a laugh. "I mean, just think: in 1699 there was no pianoforte, not as we know it, and more importantly, no tuning fork!" she said merrily.

Elizabeth laughed. "True, true: what else, Izzy?" she asked gaily, as though her sister in law were some kind of fortune teller and this was a lovely new game.

"Well perhaps by 1899 we shall have a way to, ummm, preserve music, and listen to it whenever we want," Izzy ventured. She'd have to be careful. It wasn't so much the idea that if she started predicting things that then came true, people would really wonder how she'd known. It was more the concept that if she said too much, particularly about the future, she might inadvertently change the course of history. And that could, it was theorized, change the future. Best to err on the side of caution.

Elizabeth frowned. "But how could we 'preserve' music to listen to later? 'Tis notes on the air, vibrations of strings and skins in the wind!"

Izzy sighed. "Well, remember that  100 years ago, we had a very small understanding of electricity," Izzy began, with a sidelong glance at Josh. "But today, we have the Leyden jar, and the lightning rod, and the electric telegraph, and we just heard—" she looked at her husband again—"of an Italian man, Alessandro Volta, who has developed a way to store electricity to use at will."

Indeed, that had been the big stumbling block with regard to electricity: people knew what it was, and even knew rudimentary uses for it. But with no way to store it and use it at specific times, there weren't a lot of applications yet.

"I think by 1899 we will see many many more inventions using electricity. Machines, for example, all kinds of machines, anything you can imagine, and lighting..." Izzy went on.

"Lighting!" exclaimed Sam, sounding shocked, but clearly also imagining the uses to which he could put electricity in his mills. Electricity to power the wheels. And electric lighting would mean safe operations nearly round the clock! That would double production, or more. What an intriguing idea.

Izzy nodded, and carried on. "At the turn of the last century, we didn't have the spinning jenny, or Mr. Johnson's dictionary," she offered. A copy of the newest dictionary had pride of place in the library of their home. "Or hot air balloons. I think we may develop more reliable means of transportation and communication, improvements on the steam engine and the telegraph. Boats that can ply the great rivers with engines of steam. Hmmm..." she wracked her brains for other things that would be invented in the new century. "Two wheeled, pedaled means of transport that will become popular with both men and women and begin to replace the horse, at least in cities," she said.

"Nothing replaces a good steed," Sam declared stoutly.

"Huh, yes, well, we'll see, won't we?" Izzy chuckled. It was too bad, she thought, that Sam wouldn't live long enough to see automobiles.

Both Sam and Elizabeth gave her doubting looks.

"We'll have much, much better ways of preserving food, ways that use lighter, metal containers and heat to process and create a vacuum to keep the food safe for years, not just for a season," she said. "And a method of making milk safe, of removing the bacteria in it," she added.

Elizabeth smiled. "'Twould be wondrous, those things: 'twould mean the end of hunger," she said softly.

Izzy nodded, but didn't tell Elizabeth that no, hunger would never be eradicated no matter what improvements in food storage were made. "And more vaccinations like the one for smallpox will be invented too," Izzy added. The smallpox vaccination was quite new still. "I think there will be many more medical advances in this new century, even things to kill infection and lessen pain—besides alcohol."

"That can only be good," Sam agreed, nodding.

"A machine may be invented that will do your sewing for you," Izzy continued, warming to her subject. She nodded to Elizabeth. "And the thread could be stronger, better, less likely to break," she added.

"How wonderful!" Elizabeth exclaimed.

Then Izzy turned back to Sam. "There might be an improvement in the makeup of rubber, making it strong and hard and tough, with many more uses," she said. "And there might be a way developed to travel from floor to floor in a building without stairs," she added, her tone mischievous.

"What, will we have moving stairs?" Sam asked incredulously.

"Perhaps, but there could also be a way to pull a—a box full of people—to upper stories, and a way to send them down safely again," Izzy explained.

Sam scoffed. "Now, you have entered the realms of fantasy, sister," he declared with a grin.

"Ah, Sam, but what else is progress, really, what else are inventions, but dreams brought to life?" Izzy asked.

# CHAPTER TWENTY EIGHT

"You were being very daring, telling Sam and Elizabeth about those things," Joshua chided Izzy gently a short while later. They had arrived safely back at the house, and he and Izzy were now in their little bedroom, whispering so as not to wake anyone. "The inventions—were they all true?" he queried, curious.

Izzy shrugged as she unhooked her gown and then loosened her stays. A sigh of relief escaped her, and she removed her jewelry and unbound her hair. "Yes, Josh," she admitted. "But as far as Lizzie and Sam know, I was just giving examples of things that *might* happen," she defended herself. "I wasn't predicting. And anyway, Lizzie and Sam wouldn't believe me even if I did predict something," she declared.

"Mmmm…mayhap," Joshua rejoined, slipping out of his own finery as he spoke. "But be careful, wife: among family, perhaps, you can get away with such fancies. But…"

"I'm usually really careful, Josh, you know that, " Izzy protested. She sighed. "It just seemed that tonight, at the start of a new century, a little predictive amusement was in order." She shook her head. "I'm sure they didn't really take anything I said seriously."

"You are probably right," Joshua admitted. "And they love you, so even if they knew…"

"Do you want to tell them, very badly?" Izzy asked hesitantly. She caught his face in her hands.

Joshua took a deep breath. "No. No, Izzy, I think the fewer people who know—the truth—the better. But you're right: many times I do think it would be so much—simpler! And sometimes, like tonight, such a special night, it is tempting to tell them, and share with them what a truly remarkable woman I am wed to," he concluded, his voice softening as he drew her close.

After New Year's Day, which was a quiet affair, nothing like the modern day extravaganzas Izzy knew from her own time, there were three more days of visiting. On one, Elizabeth and Izzy were out in the carriage making calls on other ladies. On the next, they were once again 'at home' and receiving visitors. And on that Saturday, they caught any last few social acquaintances they hadn't had a chance to pay a call on.

There was great emphasis on making whatever calls they could during the fortnight holiday period. Not only was it tradition, but with the typically harsh winters in the northeast of the country, most visiting as well as other social events were put on hold until spring. So now was the time to enjoy ones neighbors and friends, because one may not see them again until the snow melted.

Izzy and Elizabeth's calls were finished by Friday mid day, so they took advantage of a clear, but cold afternoon to travel into Wyalusing. Elizabeth, in particular, wished to visit Mrs. Charney and obtain more of her tea.

Izzy convinced Elizabeth to make the journey on horseback rather than in a carriage, saying the fresh air would do them both good, and that it might be one of the last times to enjoy the weather for a while.

Surprisingly, she also convinced Elizabeth to wear her most fully skirted—and oldest—dress, and to ride astride, something Elizabeth had never done. Although Izzy had by now mastered the art of side saddle, she explained that she preferred the security of riding astride, particularly for a ten mile jaunt in the winter.

She also wore an older dress that had a very full skirt, and thus the two of them set off, bonneted and gloved, with long capes draping them so completely that no one could tell they were riding in a scandalous fashion, unless they really looked closely.

"If anyone asks, I'll tell them it's the done thing in Virginia, and I convinced you to try it," Izzy breathed as they set off. "Make it my fault."

Elizabeth laughed, but agreed, and noted wryly that wearing the fuller, older dress was a good thing, because Martha had just begun the laundry, and with all the visiting, and the ball, and then more visiting, she was down to this, her last dress and her oldest chemise.

Izzy had seen Belinda and Becky helping Martha to set up the large cauldron off to one side of the house just that morning. Into the bubbling vat of soap and water they would put everyone's undergarments: leggings, stockings, chemises, shirts, anything white that needed to be washed. The water, Izzy had observed, had been liberally sprinkled with herbs and flower petals, to make the laundered clothes smell good.

Later, she knew, the garments would be hung out to dry in the mid day sun while a second batch of washing—this time cotton garments and other sturdy materials—would go into the pot. Meanwhile, both Becky and Belinda had been dry brushing the dirt out of any garment that required it, and Belinda had shown Becky her mistress' method of removing odors and stains from the underarms of silk or wool clothing.

The key was to wash affected garments as soon as possible after they had been worn, before the stain 'set.' Only the underarms, or any other areas that had suffered stains or dirtying, were washed, not the whole garment. Belinda used warm water and a very little bit of soap to help 'move' the stain. She explained that the heat combined with the soap helped to dissolve the chemical bonds that created the stain on the garment. For very stubborn stains, a dilute mixture of vinegar and water could bring results, but one had to be careful not to overdo and either fade, or further stain, the fabric. Very thorough rinsing followed, and then a complete airing, and the garment was almost as good as new.

The trip to Mrs. Charney's little dwelling north and east of Wyalusing Village was successful, and Elizabeth obtained a good supply of the tea, which she secreted in a pannier strapped to her mount.

Then, the two women took the opportunity to call on one or two friends who lived in that village. Both were older women who had been in the Reverend Sturdevant's congregation before infirmity had rendered them virtually house bound. Hoping they would have time to make these visits, Elizabeth had brought along some of Martha's cherry jam as gifts to the elderly ladies.

As before, everyone was delighted to welcome Izzy, the still mysterious stranger who now lived in Charlottesville and knew, they supposed, all the greatest people in the land. At both homes, other women from Wyalusing who were largely strangers to Elizabeth and Izzy were making their own rounds of holiday visits and calls. Izzy thought to herself how remarkable it was that in this time, a distance of a dozen miles could mean a real lack of communication, whereas in her own day, it was nothing.

It was pleasant to visit the elderly women, who were equally delighted. They seemed just slightly shocked that Elizabeth and Izzy had ridden horses rather than taken their carriage, but Izzy breezily invoked her desire to take as much fresh air in as she could before the long return trip to Charlottesville, shut up in a carriage, and everyone seemed to accept that.

If they noticed the Sturdevant women's unorthodox mounts and dismounts, no one said a word.

Talk revolved around the social goings on of the holidays, the exceptionally cold but fine weather, and everyone's health. An outbreak of tuberculosis, or 'consumption,' north of the village was a concern.

"Has anyone tried garlic to cure it?" Izzy asked quietly.

Five pairs of eyes stared at her. Elizabeth just looked down into her tea cup.

"Garlic?" one of the women from Wyalusing asked.

Izzy nodded, and said that 'in Charlottesville' there was an excellent herbalist and homeopathic physician, who swore by garlic for many illnesses, because it was powerful against infections. She didn't dare use the word 'antibacterial' because it hadn't been invented yet. She added that the recommendation was to boil a head of garlic in water to make garlic syrup, then add this to milk and drink a little bit morning and evening. "The milk helps to coat the throat and keep the garlic where it can help the most," she finished.

"Well, that was certainly enlightening," Elizabeth remarked as, stuffed with cakes and tea, the ladies rode back, taking time to admire the late afternoon landscape. The sun's slanted rays made the shadows long, blue and deep while everything the light touched turned gold.

"Mmmm...oh, you mean my advice about garlic for consumption?" Izzy asked innocently. "Well, it's true: it can help."

Elizabeth just shook her head. "I have no doubt, Izzy, but honestly, the topics you seem to know about! You must have had a great deal of time to read in King Louis' library, and you have a wonderful memory to retain it all!" she declared.

Izzy just shrugged. "If it helps someone..."

"Oh, yes, of course," Elizabeth agreed quickly. "'Tis merely that you do seem to have quite an extensive store of knowledge."

Izzy made no comment as they continued to ride. Sometimes she, too, was tempted to tell all.

"Artists love this time of day, "Izzy said a short while later to Elizabeth as they started up the big hill that would come to be known as Kinney Heights. "The light has such a remarkable quality. They call it *l'heure bleu* in France," she added, "the 'blue hour.'"

Elizabeth nodded in agreement and the dark and light barred turkey tail feathers in her bonnet swayed with the movement. "It has always been my favorite time of day," she said.

When they reached the summit, they let the horses rest for a couple of minutes, and they looked around them. They could see across the river to the area that would be called Quick's Bend, and beyond that, to the small settlement of Sugar Run. The sky was still clear, but the sun was dropping at a alarmingly precipitous rate, and the two women hastened their mounts onward, anxious to reach home.

## CHAPTER TWENTY NINE

Ann-Lucy Sturdevant and the Reverend had invited Sam, Elizabeth, Josh and Izzy to their house in Black Walnut for a festive Twelfth Night dinner and evening the next day, Saturday. The boys' sisters would be visiting from their own homes farther afield then, too, so the event would also be a reunion of sorts.

The last of the laundry that hadn't dried outside in the brisk breeze and sunshine on Friday was brought inside and dried in front of the two Keeping Room fireplaces. Izzy was thankful to note that her wardrobe had pretty much been restored to its state upon the commencement of her journey, so she would be making the return trip, at least, with clean clothes. The children's things had also been cleaned and washed, as had Josh's, and since the Saturday invitation was a family event, Sam and Elizabeth would bring John and Peter, and Izzy and Josh would bring Nicholas and Cordelia.

Izzy especially wanted her children to look their best: this was not only the first time their larger family would be seeing them, it might be one of the few times in their lives, or at least in their childhoods, that this would happen.

She dressed Nicholas in his 'best' outfit: a newly popular 'skeleton suit,' which consisted of ankle length trousers that buttoned onto a shirt jacket. The jacket went over a shirt that had a wide ruffled collar. It was pure white, and the suit was a medium blue.

Cordelia, at ten months of age, was less of a challenge: Izzy dressed her in a white wool frock sprigged with embroidered flowers and accented with a wide pink satin sash. Her tiny cap was all lace.

There was a moment of strife when John, who was a few months older than Nicholas, protested that his younger cousin was wearing 'trousers' while he was not: Elizabeth had put her older child in his best smock and a pair of leggings, typical clothing for a little boy of three at that time.

"They're not trousers," Izzy reassured John, but offered to change Nicholas into a smock and leggings if it would avert bad feeling. Thanking her silently, Elizabeth offered to change her nephew's garments, while Izzy finished up getting Peter into his own smock and leggings.

Finally, they were ready, and they all set off in the big carriage, children on their parents' laps and the horses' bridle bells jingling merrily.

"You look sad, Izzy," Josh whispered to her as the carriage trundled down the road. Black Walnut and his father's home was a mere five miles away, but in the carriage, the trip would take about an hour.

Izzy sighed and gave her husband a small smile. "I am, a little. The horses' bells sound almost mournful to me: our visit here is nearly concluded," she explained. "This is our last, well, our last party, before we leave Monday."

"And you are so distressed to be returning to Charlottesville and our life?" Josh asked, his voice teasing, but with a note of concern nonetheless.

"No, no: I love our life," Izzy replied. "But I shall miss everyone here. Especially Lizzie," she added, and to her own surprise, her voice cracked.

"Aye: you two have always been very close, and now, you are even closer, I should wager, are you not?" Josh asked sympathetically.

Blinking back a tear, Izzy nodded. She glanced over to Elizabeth, who sat with Sam's arm around her shoulders, John sleeping with his head in her lap and Peter in her arms. Her best friend, really, she thought. She wished that somehow she could take her picture, now, just as she was.

But of course, she couldn't: she had left her wonderful iPhone and all her other twenty first century gadgets locked in their special cupboard in the master bedroom at their Charlottesville house.

And even if she'd had her iPhone with her…

She sighed. They'd be at the Reverend Sturdevants' soon: she'd better cheer up!

Ann-Lucy had pulled out all the stops, it seemed, and laid on a feast that compared favorably to the Christmas Dinner they had all enjoyed a week or so before. The Sturdevants were welcomed with mugs of hot mulled cider, perfect for warding off the chill of the day.

Then Izzy and Josh introduced their children to the rest of their paternal family: Aunt Ruth and her husband Liverius Dunning, who lived in Connecticut; Aunt Phebe and her husband Joshua Keeney and their three little girls Laura, Amy and Betsey. There was also Aunt Olive and her husband and children, Aunt Elizabeth who lived with her husband and family in Montrose; Aunt Anna and her husband David Lake, along with their daughters Electa, Laura, and Ruth. Finally, there was Aunt Sarah, who had recently married Jacob Gray and moved to New York State, and was expecting their first child. Uncle Jesse they had already met, since he had been a visitor at his brother's home during the holidays.

"Seems like it's been a busy year for the Sturdevants," Izzy joked to Josh as they finished the rounds of introductions.

He looked puzzled for a moment, but then his eye fell on his three obviously pregnant sisters, for in addition to Sarah, Anna and Phebe would also give birth in the coming year. "Aye," was all he said, but

Izzy thought he looked somehow quite smug at the thought of the Sturdevant fecundity.

The dining table had had both of its extension leaves put in, but still there would not be room for everyone. So, taking a leaf from Elizabeth's book, Ann-Lucy had created a 'children's table' in their Keeping Room, where dinner for the small fry would be supervised by their various servants.

Meanwhile, the upstairs dining room offered gleaming pure white china against a highly polished mahogany table and fine glass goblets. A few sprigs of greenery wound around the simple silver candelabra that lit the table, and the sterling flatware gleamed prettily.

But it was the food that was the real star: they began with a rich beef and onion soup followed by pickled eels and herring. Then there was suckling pig that had been roasted over a specially dug pit in the side yard. "That was Jesse's idea," the Reverend Sturdevant said of the pig roast, but he took two slices of the crispy-skinned treat nonetheless.

"Oh my goodness that's delicious!" Izzy exclaimed of the pig. "I've never had that before."

Mutton chops followed, along with baked Hubbard squash, baked beans, sweet potatoes in maple syrup, and a dish of baked green peas that was similar to the 'mushy peas' Izzy had eaten on visits to modern-day England.

Dessert followed: Chess Tarts, peach pie, a vanilla cake, and then all manner of dried fruits and nuts.

When Ann-Lucy rose to signal that the ladies should withdraw, Izzy wasn't sure she could get up, she'd eaten so much.

"I'll just waddle into the parlor with you, shall I?" Izzy whispered to Elizabeth as the two made their way together. Elizabeth giggled.

"'Twas a very fine dinner," Izzy said, loudly enough so that Ann-Lucy heard her, and smiled.

"I am so happy you enjoyed it, my dear," their hostess said happily.

Ann-Lucy had re-done the parlor in a soothing pale blue egg wash on the walls, and braided rugs in darker blues decorated the wide planked polished hardwood floor. Paintings of birds, and a couple of landscapes were hung on the walls, and several candelabra as well as two oil lamps made the space bright. A cheery fire crackled beneath a light grey marble mantel and comfortable chairs and settees were placed to encourage conversation.

The ladies sipped their tea and talked of children, the weather, sewing projects and fashion.

To a lady, they agreed that the current Regency fashion suited them very well, although Ruth noted that at times the sheerness of the muslin dresses popular in warmer weather made her feel positively scandalous. They deferred to Izzy as the arbiter of current fashion, and inquired about the newest 'looks' for the new century.

"Turbans are quite popular, especially in the evening," Izzy noted, adding that she owned a couple herself. "And plumes, of course."

"Oh, well, I like feathers, Ann-Lucy said. "But I am not sure about turbans."

"Well, 'tis just another sort of hat, is it not?" asked Sarah with a smile.

The men, Izzy knew, were talking politics, and interested as she was in the ladies' topics, she genuinely wished to be at the dining room table, at least listening to if not joining in with the gentlemen's discussion.

Then, Ann-Lucy surprised her.

## CHAPTER THIRTY

"Mrs. Joshua Sturdevant," Ann-Lucy began formally to Izzy.

"Oh, do call me Izzy, everyone does," Izzy broke in. "And we are, after all, family," she added sweetly.

Ann-Lucy looked nonplussed for a second, then blinked rapidly a few times and swallowed. "Thank you, Izzy, and you must call me Ann-Lucy," she said in return.

Izzy smiled.

"Well, Izzy, what I was going to say was, you quite possibly know more than any of us about what is really taking place in Philadelphia, and Washington."

"Ummm...yes, I suppose," Izzy began hesitantly.

"Oh, yes, Mrs. Sturdevant, who do you think will be the next President?" asked Phebe eagerly.

"I'm not..." Izzy began, but was interrupted by Sarah, who said:

"I do not like President Adams. I do not trust him since that ridiculous affair in France. Imagine, trying to keep details and facts from the American people!" she said, sounding quite fierce.

"Will Mr. Jefferson stand?" asked Anna as she sipped at a cup of tea.

"I believe so," Izzy finally was able to reply, cautious.

"I was sorry he did not defeat President Adams four years ago," put in Sarah, her tone confidential, but every capped head in the room nodded in agreement.

"And tell me, Izzy, do you think poor Mr. Jefferson will ever marry again?" Ann-Lucy asked, her tone sympathetic.

Well, of course, it would be, Izzy realized as she digested the question: Ann-Lucy was herself the Reverend Sturdevant's third wife, so she was all too familiar with the need of a widower for a new wife.

However, Izzy was not entirely sure that Jefferson had a need to re-marry. Not only did she know from her own time about Jefferson's unconventional relationship with Sally Hemings, the man himself had intimated as much to them during one of their private dinners, and Izzy had even seen a woman she was certain had been Sally, from time to time at Monticello.

Sally had a male child who was not yet two years old, and a newborn daughter, and Izzy had seen them, too, with their mother. Although Jefferson never said he had fathered either child, their red hair was something of a giveaway, particularly since Sally's hair was black although racially she was a 'high yellow' who was more Caucasian than African American. Jefferson's hair, of course, was red.

Jefferson's children by his late wife, Martha and Mary, were both married now, so he had no need of a new wife to be *in loco parentis*. And since he appeared to enjoy a healthy physical relationship with Sally Hemings, Jefferson had no need of a new wife to answer that need.

But Izzy thought that she could hardly divulge all this personal information because Jefferson would expect her to keep his confidences. So instead, she smiled at Ann-Lucy and shook her head.

"I am not sure, Ann-Lucy, for Mr. Jefferson is very content with his life as it is," she answered obliquely.

"We have heard that he has an—arrangement—with one of his black slaves," put in Ruth, and her tone was censorious.

"I heard she was quite fair," Phebe piped up. "Her father was alleged to have been Mr. Jefferson's own wife's father."

Ruth gave her sister an appraising look. "Mayhap," she conceded, but Izzy thought that Ruth wouldn't approve of the situation, no matter how light skinned the woman in question might be.

It was not considered ill use at the time for Masters to have intimate relations with their slaves.

In fact, unless the relationship was a violent or abusive one, it was more or less considered the norm. And even in the case of violence or abuse, it was not considered by most to be any cause for alarm.

Therefore, for a prominent plantation owner to be in a relationship with an attractive member of his staff really didn't excite much controversy. Except that the man in question was Thomas Jefferson. And that his wife had ostensibly been the half sister of his now alleged mistress.

Everyone turned to Izzy, the unspoken question hanging in the room: was it true? Did she know?

Izzy looked in turn at each of the women gathered with her in the room. In their pretty dresses of deep jewel tones or soft pastels, with their lacy white caps, they presented a beautiful picture of early Regency womanhood, and again Izzy wished she had her iPhone, and that she could somehow snap a photo.

She shook her head again. "I—I really cannot say," she murmured.


"We heard yesterday that the Dutch East India Company has dissolved," said Joshua Keeney, cracking a walnut and popping it in his mouth. He sat with the rest of the men at the dining room table, over which his father in law Reverend Samuel Sturdevant, presided. He added that he'd heard the news at the tavern: a traveler from Philadelphia had learned of the dissolution there, and had told anyone and everyone he met.

"Well, they have had a great deal of competition in the past decade, especially from Brazil's inexpensive sugar farmers," replied the Reverend. "They were drummed out of several countries they had controlled before, too."

"I wonder if it was not the fact that they operated out of Batavia," offered David Lake. "Maybe that was effective a century ago, but in the past two decades, surely, shipping things through Batavia before distributing it to consumers meant more transport costs!"

Sam nodded. "And you must have heard of the Company's personnel problems," he said. It was an open secret that salaries in the Company were very low, which encouraged what Izzy would have called 'black marketeering.' This, as well as the general dissatisfaction of the workers and a high mortality rate among employees also contributed to the Company's demise.

"And they were too free with their dividends," added Reverend Sturdevant, explaining that for years the Company's dividends had exceeded their profits, a situation that the Company addressed by borrowing money. Eventually, this resulted in the reduction of their net assets to zero. The Anglo Dutch Wars and the massacres of unemployed Chinese sugar traders also wreaked havoc on the Company but it had finally given up and declared bankruptcy when its charter expired at the end of 1799.

The men's talk veered from the troubles of the Company to the happier topic of business in Braintrim and surroundings. Sam brought up the possibility of buying land across the river and of starting up a ferry service once more.

"Is that something you might like to try your hand at?" he asked his younger brother Jesse.

Jesse looked intrigued, and delighted, for he very much idolized his oldest brother.

## CHAPTER THIRTY ONE

Sunday was a solemn and somewhat sad day, as Josh and Izzy spent most of it packing up everything they had brought and the gifts they'd received, in readiness for their journey home. They would leave very early the following day and follow the same route they had taken on the inbound journey, changing teams of horses as they traveled. They hoped to reach Charlottesville by the end of January.

Elvira and Caroline Goldner were the only callers on Sunday, for the entire community knew that the Joshua Sturdevants would be vastly occupied. But the Goldners had brought the shawl Izzy had requested in a rainbow of pastels, and a second shawl done in tones of cream, pink, peach and red, that they hoped she would use to show merchants in Charlottesville what they were producing. They had also brought a third shawl—Izzy wondered when they had had the time to make all three—in the soft blues and greens Elizabeth favored, for her.

After dinner, the boys seemed restive: Nicholas knew, of course, that he would be leaving the next morning and his cousins John and Peter seemed to understand, too, that a long journey was ahead of the little boy and his infant sister. Izzy tried to amuse the children with the newfangled coloring books, but they did not hold their interest, although they had in previous days. Everyone was on edge, everyone was anticipating the next morning's departure and the children felt that tension, and so would not settle to one thing or the other.

"They need to burn off some energy," Izzy noted to Elizabeth. They had all gathered in the front parlor, for Elizabeth had said she did not feel like playing or singing, and in any case, it was very chilly and so easier to keep warm in a smaller room.

Josh and Sam, the latter with his pipe and both with small glasses of port, looked over at her.

"'Tis dark, and 'tis cold: what would you have them do?" asked Sam, bemused.

"I know! They could play hide and go seek!" she announced.

Nicholas, John and Peter were familiar with the game, and so for a while they all took turns being 'it' and chasing each other around the house.

Then John lisped to his Aunt, "will you play with us?" and Izzy could not find it in her heart to refuse him, even though these last hours with Elizabeth and Sam were so precious to her.

Izzy agreed, and had a mighty challenging time of it, squeezing into cupboards and behind furniture since she was so much taller than the little boys, and had many fewer spots in which she could hide.

She was just about to tell the three boys that they would be on their own to continue to play, for she was finished, when Peter gleefully discovered her kneeling behind a settee.

"You 'it' Auntie, you 'it!'" he crowed, pointing at her with a stubby finger and jumping up and down.

"All right. One more time, I'll hide, and after that if you boys want to continue to play, you're on your own," she declared, smiling as Peter was joined by Nicholas and John.

"But we like playing with you, Aunt Isabeau," John told her solemnly.

"Thank you, John. But I want to visit with your parents, you see, for this is our last night here," Izzy replied gently. "All right?"

The boys nodded.

"All right. Now, cover your eyes and count to— erm—can you count to twenty? No? Ten again, then, but count very slowly: I want to make it a really good one so you won't find me easily!" Izzy declared merrily.

The boys covered their eyes where they all stood in what Izzy called the 'River Room.' Izzy tiptoed out, and down the stairs, careful not to make any of them creak as she did so, for by now she knew every tread.

Becky was helping Belinda finish off the packing upstairs, and Martha and Ephraim were in the Keeping Room. Martha had, unusually for her, let a round of bread scorch as she was toasting it in the fire; she had opened one of the front windows wide, and stood before it, flapping her apron to send the burned odor out of the house. Ephraim was reading, his chair drawn close to the fire against the draft. They both looked up as Izzy appeared silently at the bottom of the stairs.

Izzy took in the blackened piece of bread sitting ignominiously on the hearth, and Martha's embarrassed face, and had grinned and shaken her head. Then she held a finger to her lips and pointed over her head to indicate the three boys who would shortly come looking for her.

Martha and Ephraim both nodded: they knew the game was going on, for Izzy had hidden under the Keeping Room table several turns before, and Peter had tried to conceal himself behind a large crock of grain a while before that.

Soundlessly, Izzy grabbed up a candle in its holder, and crept to the right of the stairs, past Martha's room and Ephraim's pallet under the steps, and eased open the door to the root cellar.

She doubted the boys would think to look for her here, but just in case they did, she shut the door behind her, then moved aside a large sack of sweet potatoes. Behind it were several pumpkins, but Izzy relocated two of them, then crouched down in the small, cleared space.

She blew out her candle.

She hoped, after a half a minute in the very cold dark, listening to the small, running footsteps overhead that told her that the boys had begun their search, that they would find her soon: the position she had taken was starting to hurt, and her teeth had begun to chatter from the cold.

"I cannot find Aunt Isabeau anywhere!" declared John to his father a short while later.

"Well, have you looked everywhere?" asked Sam. He had been grateful to Izzy for suggesting the game which had kept the children occupied and which hopefully would tire them out so they would sleep. He'd been deep in conversation once more with his twin and his wife, however, and his son's interruption had distracted him.

John nodded solemnly.

"We looked upstairs, too, even though we did not think she would have gone there, because Cordelia is sleeping," Nicholas offered, coming to stand next to his cousin.

"I look under the beds," said Peter then, joining the other two.

"Well, have you looked in the Keeping Room?" Josh asked logically.

The boys nodded.

"Look again," urged Elizabeth with a smile. "And if you don't find her, call 'olly olly oxen free' and she'll come out. And then, I think, 'twill be time for bed for you three," she added, tousling John's blond hair.

The boys smiled, then turned, left the parlor, went through the River Room, and clattered down the stairs to the Keeping Room.

"We cannot find Aunt Isabeau, and mother says we must," John informed Martha in desperation. "We have looked here, though," he added, sounding desolate as he looked around the room.

Peter and Nicholas were once again peering under the table and behind big crocks and into the recesses of the rear fireplace which was empty at the moment.

"Well, I do not think you have searched everywhere," Ephraim told the boys with an arch look.

John frowned.

Ephraim jutted his chin and waggled his brows towards the little hallway where his mother's room was and where his own quarters were.

John suddenly looked inspired, and rushed to the cold larder that held meats and such. He unlatched the door and held his candle high, but saw only sides of beef hanging on overhead hooks, various other foodstuffs, and a few containers: no Aunt Izzy.

Then he moved to the root cellar door. By now, his brother and cousin had joined him. John opened the door and again held his candle high, but the room was empty, except for sacks of potatoes, piles of pumpkins, and squash of various types on a low bench.

"Mama?" called Nicholas from behind John. "Mama, are you in here?"

"Olly olly oxen free," sang out Peter.

"Come out, Aunt Isabeau," entreated John.

"Oh, come now, boys, what are you playing at?" Martha said. Having sufficiently aired out the Keeping Room, she had closed the window and fastened the shutters once more, and now came up behind the boys at the door to the root cellar.

"Mama is not here," announced Nicholas.

"But she must be," Martha replied with a shake of her head and an admonishing look. She had watched Izzy enter the root cellar and had not seen her emerge.

The Sturdevants' housekeeper moved past the children and stepped into the root cellar, an oil lamp held high.

"Madame Sturdevant?" she called as she peered beneath and behind and around the items in the small, closet like space. "Madame?"

But there was no answer, and Martha did not see Izzy, although two pumpkins appeared to be out of place, sitting atop the others and leaving a bare patch of packed earth and straw.

"Mama?" called Nicholas. "Où es tu allé?" Where have you gone?

**FINIS**

www.ingramcontent.com/pod-product-compliance
Lightning Source LLC
Chambersburg PA
CBHW022033240626
47154CB00007B/2381